CAUGHT IN THE MIDDLE

Phoebe got up when she saw The Fabulous Five coming out of the building. "Seen enough for one day?" she asked.

"I have," said Jana. "I'm exhausted. You guys must be, too."

"I'm going to take a bus directly home," said Eleanore, dusting off the seat of her jeans.

"We'll see you tonight at Montague's, won't we?" asked Christie. The London girls assured her they would. She hoped her two sets of friends would try to get to know one another tonight. She was getting pretty stressed out over trying to keep both groups happy.

"Thanks for coming with us," called Katie as the two groups headed off on their separate ways. "It was fun."

Christie winced as she heard Nicki say sarcastically, "Yeah, it was a ball."

THE FABULOUS FIVE

The Fabulous Five Together Again

BETSY HAYNES

A BANTAM SKYLARK BOOK®
NEW YORK • TORONTO • LONDON • SYDNEY • AUCKLAND

RL 5, 009–012

THE FABULOUS FIVE TOGETHER AGAIN
A Bantam Skylark Book / May 1992

ISBN 0-553-15968-2

Published simultaneously in the United States and Canada

*Bantam Books are published by Bantam Books, a division of Bantam Double-
day Dell Publishing Group, Inc. Its trademark, consisting of the words
"Bantam Books" and the portrayal of a rooster, is Registered in U.S. Patent
and Trademark Office and in other countries. Marca Registrada. Bantam
Books, 666 Fifth Avenue, New York, New York 10103.*

PRINTED IN THE UNITED STATES OF AMERICA
CWO   0 9 8 7 6 5 4 3 2 1

The Fabulous Five Together Again

CHAPTER

1

Christie Winchell's heart pounded as she stood near the customs area at London's Gatwick International Airport. "They should be here any minute," she said eagerly to her dad and three British friends, Phoebe Mahoney, Nicki McAfee, and Eleanore Geach, who were waiting with her. The plane that was bringing Jana Morgan, Katie Shannon, Melanie Edwards, and Beth Barry, Christie's best friends from the United States, had landed a short time ago, and Christie thought she would absolutely die if they didn't show up soon. She had been waiting so long for this moment. Finally spring break had arrived, and now they had a whole week together to do everything that Christie had planned.

It seemed as if more than just a few months had passed since Christie's father had been transferred to London, England, and her family had moved to a flat on Queen's Pudding Square in the Bloomsbury District. So much had happened to her since then.

At first Christie had been lonely and over-whelmed. England was a lot like America, but some things were totally different. For instance, here a "cove" meant a guy, and a "child-minder" was a baby-sitter. Private schools such as St. Margaret's, where Christie went, were called "public schools." There had been times, too, when Christie thought she would never find friends. But then she'd met Phoebe, Nicki, and Eleanore, who reminded her a lot of her friends in The Fab Five. Since then, she hadn't felt nearly as lonely. In a few minutes her two groups of friends would finally meet. Christie couldn't wait. She knew they would all like each other as much as she liked all of them.

Suddenly a man pushing a luggage cart piled high with suitcases emerged from customs. As other passengers followed, Christie stood on tiptoe and craned her neck to see. Just as she was beginning to think her friends had missed the plane, she saw Beth and Melanie pushing a cart loaded with their be-longings. Jana and Katie were a few feet behind them, struggling to keep their suitcases from falling off their cart. A flight attendant was helping.

"*There they are!*" Christie screamed, pounding on Phoebe's arm in her excitement.

"You'd think the Queen herself was arriving the way you're carrying on," Nicki said in her sarcastic way. "They're not being raised from the dead, you know."

"I know," said Christie, waving frantically to get The Fabulous Five's attention. "But wait till you meet them. Then you'll know why I'm so excited. Beth! Melanie! Over here!"

"*CHRISTIE!*" shrieked Melanie and Beth in unison. They steered their luggage cart toward her, charging madly through the crowd of other passengers. Katie and Jana saw Christie, too, and soon Christie was enveloped in hugs from her best friends.

Phoebe, Nicki, and Eleanore stood watching, and Mr. Winchell went to the flight attendant to identify himself as the person who was meeting the girls.

Tears streamed down Christie's face. "I've missed you all so much," she whispered as she hugged each of The Fab Five in turn.

"And we didn't miss *you* at all," teased Jana, beaming at Christie. "We never talked about you— except for all the time."

"You look the same!" exclaimed Katie. "But you sound a little different. You've got a British accent!"

"What did you expect, mate?" asked Christie, laughing. "I'm a British bird now."

"Hey, there's your dad," exclaimed Katie. "Hi, Mr. Winchell!" She waved, and he motioned for them to follow him to an exit.

"Come on," said Beth, pulling the strap to her carry-on over her shoulder. "Let's get out of here." As she turned to push her cart, Nicki had to step back to keep from being run over.

"Oops, sorry," Beth called over her shoulder, continuing on her way before Christie had a chance to introduce Nicki.

"Did your father bring a truck to haul all our stuff to your house?" asked Katie.

Christie laughed. "No, but he did rent a van. Oh, I want you to meet . . ." She started to introduce her London friends, but before she could finish, Katie, Melanie, and Jana headed after Beth.

"Excuse me," Melanie said to Phoebe as she squeezed past her.

"Quite all right," replied Phoebe, moving out of the way.

"A bit rude, if you ask me," muttered Nicki.

Christie pretended she hadn't heard, and she was glad that Melanie hadn't caught the remark.

"Could you grab my purse, Christie?" asked Jana. "I've got more than I can handle. It took customs forever to go through all our stuff."

As Christie grabbed Jana's bag, Katie and Melanie

immediately started firing questions at her about what they were going to do while they were in England.

Christie glanced over her shoulder at her London friends. They were trailing behind The Fabulous Five, looking a bit lost. Abruptly she ran to the front of The Fabulous Five's parade of carts.

"Hey, everybody, *STOP*!" she said, holding up a hand.

The Fabulous Five froze.

"What's wrong?" asked Jana, looking astonished. Then she noticed Phoebe, Nicki, and Eleanore for the first time. "Uh-oh." She put her hand over her mouth. "Are you who I think you are?" she asked the London girls.

"I've been trying to tell you," said Christie. "This is Eleanore, Nicki, and Phoebe."

"Oh, wow," said Katie, looking embarrassed. "I didn't even see you."

"Yeah," mumbled Beth. "We were so excited about seeing Christie, we didn't notice you."

"That's understandable," said Eleanore warmly.

Nicki grinned. "But a bit airy-fairy."

"Huh?" Beth looked puzzled.

"Hush your cake hole, McAfee," said Phoebe. "Pay her no mind," she told Beth. "I'm happy to meet you, and Nicki is, too."

"As am I," chimed in Eleanore. "Actually Christie has told us so much about you, I feel as if I know you already."

Christie smiled as her two sets of friends began talking. Even though things hadn't started out well between them, she just knew they would all be great buddies before long. This was going to be a wonderful vacation!

CHAPTER

2

"*H*ave we got everything?" asked Mr. Winchell as he tied the last knot in the rope holding The Fabulous Five's luggage on top of the van.

"How long have you come to stay, anyway?" asked Nicki as she looked at the towering pile of suitcases. "I don't think St. Meg's has room for four new students next semester."

"I'm not sure I'd fit in at your school," answered Beth with a laugh. "For one thing, I don't know what airy-fairy means, although I can guess what a cake hole is."

"Okay, everybody," said Mr. Winchell. "Time to get cozy."

Christie got into the passenger seat next to her

father, while everyone else squeezed into the two bench seats in the back.

"We're going to have so much fun," said Christie, twisting in her seat so she could talk to the others. "We'll definitely go to the Tower of London, and to Soho to shop. And Trevor Morgan's group, Brain Damage, is doing an outdoor concert in Hyde Park. It's a beautiful place. We'll get tickets for that. And Connie Farrell—he's the boy I told you about whose family is royalty—says he wants all of us to go horseback riding at their estate near Hoddesdon. I just can't wait to show you all the great things there are to do in London."

"Maybe we'll get to talk to Trevor," said Beth. "Do you think he'll remember us?"

Katie laughed. "After the trick you pulled on him with the Indian costume, how could he forget us?"

"You know Trevor Morgan?" asked Phoebe, her eyes widening in surprise.

"Oh, yes," replied Melanie. "Would you believe the five of us sang onstage with him? That was after Beth spread a rumor that Jana was related to him."

The girls all laughed, and Mr. Winchell cocked an eyebrow. It was the first time he was hearing the story, too.

"We want to show you the Montague Youth Club," said Christie. "That's where everyone hangs out, isn't it?" She looked to the London girls for confirmation.

"Yes, it is," agreed Phoebe. "We go there on weekends with our chums. Lots of fellas hang out there, and you can dance or play arcade games."

Melanie's face brightened at the mention of boys, as usual. "I can't wait to meet some blokes," she commented, faking a British accent.

The British girls laughed.

"Isn't that what you call boys?" asked Melanie.

"Not too often," replied Eleanore. "We mostly call them coves or fellas."

"Montague's sounds neat," said Jana. "We go to a place called Bumpers all the time. It's a fast-food restaurant with old bumper cars used as booths. All the kids from Wacko, that's what we call Wakeman Junior High, go there after school. Sometimes we go there at night after movies, too."

"And then there's Mama Mia's pizzeria," chimed in Katie. "We go there sometimes."

"And the mall," added Beth. "We usually spend the *whole* weekend hanging out there. Don't you miss all those places, Christie?"

Tears immediately sprang into Christie's eyes. She mumbled yes and turned quickly to face out the side window so the others wouldn't see.

The truth was, she did miss all those places and

the wonderful times she had had there with The Fabulous Five. Sometimes those memories were just too painful. She wiped the tears away and then turned around to face her friends again. The only thing that mattered right now was that The Fabulous Five were together again, and nothing could make Christie happier.

When they pulled in front of the building the Winchells lived in on Queen's Pudding Square, Christie's mother came down the front steps to meet them. Mr. Dudley, the building caretaker, popped up from the stairs outside the basement.

"I'm so glad you girls could come," said Mrs. Winchell, hugging each of them.

"Welcome, lasses," called Mr. Dudley, pulling suitcases off the van. "Christie told me her friends from the States were coming. It's nice to have you young holiday-makers here."

"*Holiday-makers?*" echoed Melanie.

"The English call going on vacation going on holiday," Christie explained, "and people on holiday are holiday-makers."

"Then what do you call holidays like Christmas?" asked Jana.

"They're holidays, too," said Eleanore, smiling. "But we go *on* holiday when we go away for fun."

"Never mind." Mr. Winchell chuckled. "We can't stand here all day discussing holidays and vacations. Let's help Mr. Dudley with your things. Christie can explain it all to you later."

"Put your suitcases in the library," directed Mrs. Winchell as the girls marched up the stairs to the second floor. "You can use it as your dressing room. There's not enough drawer space in Christie's room."

"I'll unpack later," said Katie, putting her bag down. "I want to see your room, Christie."

"Me, too," said Beth. "From what you said in your letters, it's fantastic."

"Follow me." Christie led the way. Phoebe, Nicki, and Eleanore trailed behind.

"Wow. Look at that," cried Melanie when she saw the giant, four-poster bed with the overstuffed mattress. "It looks so soft. Can we take turns sleeping on it?"

"Two at a time," said Christie's mother. "We've also got three sleeping bags. Christie insisted that you sleep in the same room, no matter how crowded it was."

"Oh, look at the bears," said Jana. "They're on the bed just like you said, Christie."

Propped against the pillows were the four bears that Jana, Katie, Beth, and Melanie had given Christie the day she had left for England. Each of the bears was meant to remind her of the giver. Melanie's bear was reddish brown, the color of Melanie's hair, and was wearing a dress with hearts all over it. Beth's had on wild, fluorescent-color clothes and was wearing sunglasses. Spiral earrings hung from its little round ears. Katie's bear looked like an English judge with a white wig and a gavel in its paw, and Jana's was dark brown, the same color as her hair. It had on a hat that said "Reporter." Christie had placed her own bear, which was dressed in a white tennis outfit, in the middle of the others.

"Remember the day you left?" asked Beth. "We cried for hours."

After a few minutes of listening to The Fabulous Five reminiscing about Christie's departure, Eleanore said, "I ought to be going."

"Me, too," said Phoebe.

"Oh, don't go," pleaded Christie. "I want you guys to get to know each other."

"We're just in the way right now," responded Nicki. "You chums have a lot of chin-wagging to do. Ring us up later when you're ready to do something."

"I will," Christie promised. "Maybe we can all go to Montague's tonight."

When the three girls had left, Jana said, "They seem nice, Christie."

"I think so, too," added Beth. "But I'm not sure

Nicki and I are as much alike as you said in your letter. She's kind of, uh . . . snippy. What's airy-fairy mean, anyway?"

"It means unreal," explained Christie.

Beth wrinkled her nose. "Unreal? Why'd she say we were unreal?"

"Oh, it was just her way of being funny," replied Christie. "You'll like her once you get to know her. Besides, I didn't mean you were *exactly* alike. But you are both kind of off the wall, and her hair is cut sort of like yours. That's what I meant."

"Do you really think Phoebe is like me?" asked Jana.

"Kind of," answered Christie. "Same hair color, and both of you are quiet and well liked."

"I have to tell you, Christie, I don't see any resemblance between Eleanore and me, either," remarked Katie.

Christie shrugged. "Forget about it," she told her friends. "It's no big deal. The three of them just reminded me of you when I first met them. Actually I was so lonely, I was probably looking for you guys in everyone I met. It's a compliment. I know you're going to like them as much as I do, when you get to know them."

Katie was silent for a few seconds. "I know you need friends here, too," she said finally. "But it's kind of strange to see you with another group."

Christie looked at her Fab Five friends. They had known each other forever. "You guys are still my best friends, but Phoebe, Nicki, and Eleanore are important to me, too. I go to school with them, and we hang out together. Now that I'm here, I need them, but they'll never replace you."

"I'm sorry I said what I did," Katie replied quickly. She grabbed Christie and hugged her. "It was dumb."

"Hey," cried Beth, grinning. "Enough already. We came to England to see Christie and have fun. Let's do it."

"Don't tell me you girls have unpacked already," said Mrs. Winchell a few minutes later when the girls came into the kitchen.

"Not completely, Mum," answered Christie, heading out the back door. "But I want to show them the courtyard first."

"Don't be long," said her mother. "Lunch is almost ready."

"I love the way you call your mother *Mum*," commented Melanie. "It's so . . . so British."

"This is nice," remarked Katie, looking around.

Several two-story brick buildings formed a wall around the parklike court. The neighbors' back doors opened onto the courtyard and had small porches covered with flowerpots and hanging plants. In the middle stood a large old tree whose long branches shaded a bench. A stone walkway skirted the court's edges, connecting the back doors.

"Well, look who has come to say hello," said Christie, bending to pick up a yellow cat that had drifted over to them. "Beth, this is Agatha. I told you about her. She lives with Mrs. Mansfield in that flat with the garden by the door."

Beth, whose family owned a large Old English sheepdog with the same name, laughed and took the cat from her.

"Where does Jenny, the little girl who thinks she's a dog, live?" asked Jana.

Christie pointed to a door across the way. "Over there. Only now she thinks she's a kitty."

"From what you said, it sounds as if Jenny's more of a tiger," said Katie.

"Believe me, she is," replied Christie. "But she's also lovable and very smart. It's funny. The Fitzhughs are so prim and proper, and Jenny is exactly the opposite. I bet one of their ancestors was a pirate or something. Jenny has to have inherited her genes from someone like that."

"What's for lunch, Mum?" asked Christie as they walked back into the Winchells' flat.

"In honor of your first day here, I thought we'd have something typically British," Mrs. Winchell told the girls. "We're having shepherd's pie."

"Pie for lunch?" exclaimed Melanie. "That's great.

My parents would never let us get away with just having dessert."

"Don't get your hopes up," warned Christie. "It's made out of meat and mashed potatoes."

"Oh," said Melanie, the look of anticipation fading from her face.

But her spirits perked up when Christie asked if everyone wanted to go to the Montague Youth Center after dinner.

"You bet," cried Melanie, and the others quickly agreed.

"Great," said Christie. "I'll call Phoebe, Nicki, and Eleanore and have them meet us there."

The Fab Five spent the rest of the afternoon in Christie's room napping and filling Christie in on what was going on at Wakeman Junior High. She asked about Chase Collins—the boy she was dating before she left—Randy Kirwan, Shane Arrington, and Tony Calcaterra. They told her all the things they could think of about what their arch-rivals, Laura McCall and her friends in The Fantastic Foursome, were pulling.

The most surprising thing they told her was that a proposal to change Wakeman from a junior high school to a middle school was being considered.

"You mean that you'd be the top class at Wakeman when you got into the eighth grade then?" asked Christie.

"That's right," answered Jana. "It's great for us, but think about all the kids who are in the eighth grade now. They thought *they'd* be the senior class next year. Instead they'd be lowly freshmen in high school."

"Garrett Boldt and Daphne Alexandrou must love that!" said Christie. "What a blow."

The others nodded and began talking excitedly about the possibility of Wakeman's becoming a middle school. Christie sat back and listened to her friends. She was happy for them, but it made her sad, too. It was one more thing going on back home that she wouldn't be a part of. She couldn't help wondering if the longer her family stayed in England, the fewer things she and The Fabulous Five would have in common.

CHAPTER

3

"**W**ow! Cool!" exclaimed Katie, taking in the interior of Montague's.

Ping-Pong tables with several couples playing matches were on the right. A row of video machines lined the wall behind them. In the center of the room was a jukebox and dance floor. Snack machines stood side by side along the wall to the left.

"Over here!" called Phoebe. She was seated with Nicki and Eleanore at several tables that had been pulled together. There were three boys with them.

"We've had a devil of a time saving chairs for you," Eleanore told them. "We could have rented them a half dozen times over."

"Thanks," said Christie. "Guys, this is Jana Morgan, Katie Shannon, Beth Barry, and Melanie Edwards. And this is Connie Farrell, Charlie Fenwick, and Davey Hopper," she said to The Fab Five.

"Welcome to London," Connie greeted them.

"The more birds, the merrier," added Charlie, lifting his soda in a salute.

"Birds?" asked Katie.

"He means girls," explained Christie.

"That's a terrible term for girls," said Katie. "It sounds so sexist. Why don't you call girls *girls*?"

"Come on, Katie," said Jana. "It doesn't make any difference."

"In the interest of good relations with our former colonies, I'll call Katie a girl, if that's what she wants to be called," Charlie said, chuckling. "But I want you to know, all the rest of you are still birds."

"We heard you personally know Trevor Morgan," said Davey. "Maybe you could five us an intro." He pulled out a seat for Melanie, and she sat down.

"If you guys get tickets to the concert and go with us, we can try," she said.

"That's an all-right idea," Davey replied. "What's your favorite Brain Damage song, Melanie?" The two of them began talking about Brain Damage music.

"What do you do for fun in the States?" Charlie asked Beth.

"Everything," she responded. "I just learned to

ski this year, and Mel and I are cheerleaders. Most of all, though, I like acting, *daahling*." She struck a dramatic pose.

"You're an actress?" asked Charlie, looking interested.

"Is she ever," replied Jana. "Beth's had the lead part in several plays at school; she's been on cable television; and a big casting director from New York said she was great."

"Well, not really *great*," said Beth modestly. "He did say I was good, though."

"I've never known a famous actress before. Would you autograph my napkin?" teased Charlie. He pushed it toward her.

"Well, I don't usually do autographs when I'm socializing," Beth joked. She patted Charlie's cheek playfully and added, "but . . . since it's *you*." She dug a ballpoint pen from her purse and signed the napkin with a flourish and gave it back to him.

"I'll keep this next to my heart forever," he told her, sticking it inside his shirt.

"Yeah, right where he can sweat on it," said Nicki.

Everyone laughed except for Eleanore, Christie quickly noticed. She had been dating Charlie recently.

"You're planning to ride at my family's country place, aren't you?" asked Connie.

"We wouldn't miss it," said Katie. "Christie has told us about Rigel, the Arabian horse you let her ride."

"He's eager to meet more Americans," Connie replied with a grin. "When can you come?"

"How about Friday?" Christie suggested. "I'm sure The Fab Five will be shopped out by then."

Beth laughed. "I won't be! But I probably will be broke." She turned to Nicki. "Speaking of shopping, where'd you get the sweater you have on? I've never seen anything like it."

Nicki's oversized sweater was bright green and had dozens of small objects attached to it. "Are those earrings?"

Nicki nodded. "I collected them for a long time and then finally had enough to fasten to the sweater."

"Beth makes great earrings out of fishing line," Christie jumped in. "She's creative like you, Nicki." She was hoping that the two girls' interest in wild clothes would make them like each other.

"Christie told us that you're the son of a baron," Katie said to Connie. "What's it like to be royalty?"

He smiled. "It's really no big deal. England is filled with people descended from royalty."

"He's just being modest," commented Phoebe. "His family is very posh."

Connie shrugged, then changed the subject.

"Friday's fine for riding." He turned to Nicki, Phoebe, and Eleanore. "Can you come, too?"

"I thought you'd never ask," said Nicki. The three girls promised to be there. As everyone began chattering away about how much fun riding would be, Christie watched Jana. Her friend seemed so quiet. Is something wrong, Christie wondered, or is it my imagination?

"Do you want to pick out a Brain Damage song on the jukebox?" Davey asked Melanie.

"Sure." Melanie hopped up from her chair.

Nicki, who was going out with Davey, kept an eye on the two of them as they walked across the dance floor together, talking and laughing.

"So?" Connie said, looking at Jana and Katie. "What great talents do you two have?"

The girls looked at each other.

"I don't know if we have any special talents," replied Katie. "I'm a judge on the Teen Court at Wakeman."

"And I'm on the yearbook staff," offered Jana.

"See, you do have talents," said Connie. "I guess that's why you're called The *Fabulous* Five."

A Brain Damage song started playing, and Melanie and Davey began to dance. Christie noticed Nicki watching them like a hawk.

"Would you dance with me?" Charlie asked Beth.

"Sure."

Nicki and Eleanore exchanged glances as Beth and Charlie made their way to the dance floor.

Just then two boys Christie had seen around the club came over to their table and asked Jana and Katie if they'd like to dance. They accepted.

"Excuse me," said Connie. "I need to say something to Dick Lasley."

When he had gone, Christie saw that Nicki and Eleanore were still watching the couples on the dance floor. "Don't worry about Melanie and Beth," she told them. "They're just having fun."

"With our coves," pointed out Nicki.

"Melanie's got a boyfriend named Shane Arrington whom she really likes," replied Christie, "and Beth wouldn't steal anyone's boyfriend. They're only being friendly. You'll see."

Nicki looked skeptical, but Eleanore smiled. "We'll see," she said.

Just then Connie came back. "How about a dance?" he asked Christie.

"Love to." She gave Nicki and Eleanore another smile of reassurance before she followed Connie.

"This is great," cried Melanie, bouncing up and down on Christie's bed later that evening. The five friends had drawn straws to see who would sleep in it first. Katie and Melanie had won.

Christie and Jana had unrolled their sleeping bags on the floor in front of the bed and were writing on postcards they had bought at a shop after leaving the youth club. Beth had placed her sleeping bag near the door. "So I won't step on anyone when I try to find my way to the bathroom in the middle of the night," she had explained.

"I'm glad I'm not afraid of heights," Katie said, peeking over the edge of the bed. "This is one high bed."

"If you want to trade places with me, I'll make the sacrifice for you," volunteered Jana.

"No way," Katie responded. "I'm going to pretend I'm the Queen of England sleeping in the imperial suite."

"With all your handmaidens sleeping around you?" joked Beth.

"Whatever," said Katie, plumping up her pillow and flopping back with a smile of contentment. "What are those ribbons for, Christie?" she asked, pointing to two blue ribbons pinned to the wall.

"Those are the ribbons I won at the science fairs," answered Christie. "One is from St. Meg's, the other is from the Bloomsbury District competition." Changing the subject, she added, "I'll be so jealous if Wakeman becomes a middle school. In the private schools here you stay in the same school until you're eighteen. It will take me forever to be part of the oldest class at school."

"Wow," said Beth. "That's terrible. Are the subjects here hard?"

Christie nodded. "The schools are tougher here. If you want to go to college, you have to start taking subjects to prepare for it when you're thirteen. And when you're sixteen, you take a comprehensive exam to see if you can get into the college you want."

"That sounds serious," said Melanie. "Do you know which college you want to go to?"

"Either Oxford or Cambridge," answered Christie.

"They're both in England, right?" asked Katie.

"Yes," Christie replied.

"You won't even be coming back to the United States to go to college?" asked Beth.

Christie shook her head.

"Isn't there any chance your father will be transferred back to the States?" asked Melanie.

Christie shrugged and looked down at her hands folded in her lap. "I doubt it," she said softly. "He hasn't been in his job long enough."

The room was filled with silent gloom. Finally Jana broke the tension. "I need to brush my teeth.

Don't talk about anything interesting until I get back."

Christie watched Jana as she left the room. "Is something bothering her?" she whispered to the others after she was gone. "She seems so distracted—or something."

Beth, Melanie, and Katie exchanged glances.

Katie nodded. "She is worried about something."

"Does it have anything to do with Randy?" asked Christie.

Randy Kirwan and Jana had been going together since elementary school, and everyone called them the perfect couple. They had even been elected Mr. and Miss Wakeman Junior High earlier in the school year.

"No." Melanie shook her head. "But it's pretty serious."

"Maybe Jana will tell you about it herself," added Beth.

When Jana returned, the talk shifted back to Wakeman Junior High and the possibility that it would be a middle school next year. As the girls talked, Christie half-listened. She still wanted to hear about kids from Wacko and what they were doing, but as time went on, she felt less and less interest. Even Chase Collins, whom she used to think of all the time, seemed far away now.

Will I ever see Chase again? Christie wondered. I'd like to . . . It would be so much fun if he visited me in London, too. We could ride up the Thames River together, or tour Soho. It would be so romantic to be together in Europe.

With a tiny stab of guilt she thought of Connie and how much she liked him. He was so nice and had been so friendly to The Fabulous Five tonight. Why did I ever have to move, anyway? Christie thought as Katie shut out the light and everyone called "Good night." Sometimes it was so confusing to have friends who lived in separate places.

CHAPTER

4

"What are we going to do today?" asked Katie the next morning as The Fabulous Five ate breakfast.

"Let's get tickets for the Brain Damage concert right away," suggested Melanie.

"Yeah," agreed Beth. "I can't wait to see them—and a play. I've *got* to see a play."

"There's a half-price ticket booth in Leicester Square," volunteered Christie's mother. She had taken a couple of days off from her job at the University of London to be at home with the girls at the start of their vacation. "And there are agencies nearby where you should be able to get tickets for the concert. From there it's an easy walk to Piccadilly Circus, where there are some good shops, like Lillywhites and Simpsons. There are lots of great shops in Soho."

"All right!" exclaimed Melanie, raising her toast into the air. "Monster shopping and a circus, too."

Mrs. Winchell chuckled. "Piccadilly Circus isn't the kind of circus you're thinking of, dear. In England they call a traffic circle a 'circus.'"

"It's a traffic circle?" Melanie said in disbelief. "How come I've heard of it, if it's just a plain old traffic circle?"

"Lots of interesting things go on there. Performers like jugglers entertain, and people often demonstrate over political causes," said Mrs. Winchell.

"One of the first things we have to do is get you travel cards," said Christie. "You'll need to take along your passports to be able to buy them."

"What are travel cards?" asked Jana.

"They're special tickets that let you take the buses or the Underground as often as you want," Christie explained. "We'll be using them a lot."

"Will we get to see Buckingham Palace?" asked Melanie. "I want to see Princess Di."

"And Old Bailey, the court where they held the trials for all those famous murderers and spies," added Katie. "I've got to see that."

"Will we be able to use our travel cards to get to Connie's place in the country?" asked Jana.

The girls' questions came faster and faster.

"*Mo-om!*" cried Christie as the girls overwhelmed her. "Help!"

Mrs. Winchell laughed. "I think you girls need to get organized," she told them. "Why don't you make a list of the things you want to see, then decide when you want to visit each one."

"Will Dad be able to take us to Connie's on Friday?" asked Christie.

"You'll have to talk to him about that, sweetheart. Some executives from the company's headquarters in the United States are here this week checking on things. He may be pretty busy. When you get your list made, we'll sit down with your father and go over it."

"Great idea," said Katie.

"Don't forget about Christie's birthday," said Mrs. Winchell. "It's Saturday, and we need to plan a special dinner for her."

"Christie's our old lady." Melanie laughed. "She's the first one to turn fourteen."

Christie stuck her tongue out at Melanie. "Your birthday's next month, Melanie Edwards, and the rest of you will be fourteen before you know it."

"First things first," declared Jana. "Let's go get tickets to Brain Damage, and we can decide what to do next."

* * *

"That was easy," remarked Jana as The Fabulous Five emerged from the Underground at the Leicester Square stop. "I wish we had subways like that at home. Everything's so clean, and there's no graffiti here. I want to ride one of those big double-decker buses," she said, pointing to one that was passing by.

"Let's get our concert tickets quickly and go to Piccadilly Circus," suggested Katie. "Maybe Melanie can ride one of the elephants there."

"Funneeey!" retorted Melanie, wrinkling her nose at Katie. She unfolded the map she was carrying so they could all see it. "Buckingham Palace doesn't look far from there. Maybe we can go there afterward."

"Don't forget shopping," Beth said. "We have to go to Soho to shop."

"All right! All right!" Christie laughed. "We'll do it all eventually. Just give me a break." She had to chuckle at her friends. They were like little kids in a candy store.

Piccadilly Circus was mobbed. Cars and buses were pouring into the circle from several side streets, and darting back out again. In the center of the circle was a statue of a man with wings holding a bow and arrow.

"Look at those people sitting around the statue," observed Jana. "Have you ever seen such wild hair and clothes? Check them out, Beth."

Several of the people had their hair moussed into

long spikes or Mohawk cuts and dyed in bright colors. Most had on black leather or torn denim jackets and pants with shiny metal studs. The boys in the crowd were wearing at least as many earrings and necklaces as the girls.

"They're punkers," said Christie.

"They look pretty wild—even to me," commented Beth.

Katie pointed to the statue. "Who's the guy with the wings?"

"It says here on the map it's Eros," replied Melanie. "Is he some ancient English guy?"

Christie put her hand over her mouth to hold back a giggle. "He's the Greek god of love, Mel. Your kind of guy."

"My gosh," said Melanie, looking at the winged statue with awe. "I've always thought there *should* be a god of love; now I know there is one."

The girls stood there for a minute, taking in all the amazing sights: a juggler, the punkers, the flood of cars and tourists from all over the world.

Suddenly Melanie turned to the others. There was a sly look in her eyes. "Christie, didn't you say that anyone can perform here?" When Christie nodded, she continued, "Well, I've just made up a cheer! How about this?"

She raised her arms and did a Flying Dutchman jump, touching her toes with her fingers.

"*Yea, Fabulous Five!*" she yelled.

People passing by smiled at her.

Katie groaned. "Melanie, don't humiliate us."

"Come on," Melanie coaxed, grabbing Beth's and Jana's hands. "Let's all do it."

"Not me," said Jana. "I'm not going to make a fool of myself."

"Come on, Katie," urged Melanie. "Christie?"

"I'll do it with you, Mel," Beth said finally.

The two of them did the cheer together, and a few people stopped to watch. Most, however, walked past without thinking twice about the girls' impromptu performance. Clearly stranger things happened in Piccadilly Circus!

After that The Fab Five devoured sandwiches and sodas they bought at a small stand-up shop, and then went to several clothing stores in Soho.

By the end of the day Christie felt exhausted but happy. It was so much fun being with her friends again. It was as if they'd never been apart.

It was almost five o'clock when they trooped back into Christie's home and collapsed on the couch and chairs in the living room.

"You certainly look as if you've had a good time," Mrs. Winchell said. "You didn't spend all your money, did you?"

"Not yet," replied Katie, grinning. "But we tried. I think we went to every store in London."

"Oh, Christie," Mrs. Winchell added. "Phoebe called a couple of times. She wants you to call when you get a chance."

"I'll do it right now." Christie got up and headed for the phone. "I'll tell her which Brain Damage concert we got tickets to so she and the others can get tickets for the same night. I'll call Connie, too, and he can talk to Davey and Charlie about it."

"Hi, Phoebe," Christie said when her friend picked up. "Mum said you called. Boy, did we have a great day! Melanie and Beth did a cheer for the crowd at Piccadilly Circus."

At that Melanie and Beth started yelling and hooting in the background.

Christie grinned and motioned for them to be quiet. "We went to Soho," she went on, "and, oh, yeah, I wanted to tell you that we got tickets for Brain Damage for Friday night."

"It sounds as if you and your chums are having great fun," said Phoebe. Her voice sounded funny.

"We are," answered Christie, wondering if something was wrong.

"We thought you were going to ring us up so we could go with you," said Phoebe. "Nicki and Eleanore were over here all morning waiting. They went home when we didn't hear from you."

"Oh . . ." Christie was caught by surprise. She

hadn't realized they had expected her to call. "I wasn't thinking," she said softly. "I'm sorry."

"I think I should warn you, Christie," Phoebe responded. "That's not the only thing bothering Nicki and Eleanore. They're not too happy about Davey's and Charlie's paying so much attention to Melanie and Beth."

Christie's heart sank. She really needed to talk to Phoebe in private. "Just a minute. Let me get on another phone," she said. "There's too much noise in here." She asked Jana to hang up the phone after she picked up the extension in the kitchen.

When Christie heard the click of the phone being put back in its cradle, she said to Phoebe, "Melanie and Beth really didn't do anything. They just talked to Davey and Charlie, and danced a couple of dances with them."

"I know," replied Phoebe, "but Nicki and Ellie are still a bit put out, especially Nicki."

"I'll call them right away," said Christie. "I don't want my two sets of best friends to be angry at each other."

Then she said as cheerfully as she could, "Tonight we're going to sit down and make up a schedule of all the things The Fabulous Five want to do while they're here. I'll give you a call and let you know what we're planning."

"That would be nice," Phoebe told her. "I'll let you get back to your chums now. Talk to you later."

"Phoebe," Christie said before she could hang up, "are you still mad at me?"

"Not any longer," she replied. "Give a call when you're ready to do the town."

As soon as they had hung up, Christie took a deep breath and punched Nicki's number into the telephone.

"Before you say anything, let me apologize for not calling to ask you guys to come with us today," Christie said when Nicki answered. "It's completely my fault."

"Well, it did get a trifle boring sitting around all morning with Phoebe and Ellie," said Nicki.

Feeling relieved at Nicki's reaction, Christie went on to explain about the concert tickets. Before hanging up, she decided to bring up Melanie's and Beth's dancing with Davey and Charlie.

"They were just being friendly," said Christie. "Melanie has a boyfriend at home, and Beth wouldn't steal *anyone's* boyfriend."

There was a moment of silence, then Christie heard Nicki chuckle. "I guess I should have realized that," Nicki said. "You wouldn't have friends who would. What I need to do, I guess, is put a leash on Davey—or blinders."

Next Christie called Eleanore to explain things and apologize. Finally she made her call to Connie.

When she was finished, she felt a little better, but she still blamed herself for the misunderstandings. It just hadn't occurred to her to invite her British friends to go with them today. After all, they had seen Piccadilly Circus and Soho hundreds of times.

CHAPTER

5

*7*hat evening The Fab Five and Christie's parents went over the list of things to do that the girls had drawn up.

"Buckingham Palace, the Tower of London, Old Bailey, and Madame Tussaud's wax museum," Mr. Winchell read aloud. "You'll love the museum. Besides the wax models of famous people, there are all sorts of torture chamber displays."

Beth looked up with a gleeful expression on her face. "All right!"

"You'll get to see the crown jewels at the Tower of London," said Mrs. Winchell. "What about the Old Curiosity Shop that Charles Dickens wrote about?

It has a lot of things about him in it. You liked that when we were there, Christie."

"Yeah, that's neat," replied Christie. "Add that to the list, Jana."

"Okay," her friend replied. "Right after having our picture taken in front of Big Ben."

"Who put down the London Hard Rock Cafe?" asked Mr. Winchell.

Melanie raised her hand. "Me. I want a T-shirt from there."

"Why don't we all go there for dinner one night," suggested Mrs. Winchell. "I've got an idea. Let's plan on having Christie's birthday dinner there."

"Great," everyone agreed.

"Hey, Dad," said Christie. "Can you take us to Connie's on Friday so we can go horseback riding?"

"Let me check with Mrs. Davies, the woman from my company who's here this week, to see what her plans are," answered her father. "She was intending to stay through the weekend, but she seems happy with what she's seen so far. She may actually go back to the States on Friday. If she does, I can take you."

"When are they going to transfer you back home, Mr. Winchell?" asked Katie.

He smiled. "Things are going well, but I can't believe I'll be transferred back any time soon."

Beth made a sour face. "Darn!" The others looked down.

"So," Christie piped up, trying to change the subject, "tomorrow we'll go to Buckingham Palace."

Katie smiled. "You'll finally get to see the palace, Mel. But then we're going to Old Bailey, too."

Later that night Christie and Jana were the first ones to arrive upstairs to get ready for bed.

"It's so much fun having you guys here," Christie said, following Jana as she went into the bathroom to wash her face. "Isn't London exciting?"

Jana nodded. "I'm having a great time."

"Are you?" Christie said. "I'm glad to hear that . . ." She hesitated. "I've been wondering if something's wrong. You seem so quiet."

Jana looked at Christie's reflection in the mirror and sighed. "I guess I'm not hiding it very well, am I? I'm worried about my father."

"What's up?" asked Christie, immediately thinking of Mr. Morgan's drinking problem, which was what had led Jana's mom to divorce him. For as long as Christie could remember he had disappointed Jana. Once in elementary school he had promised to take Jana on a vacation out west, then never showed up.

"I got a letter from him," Jana explained. "He said he'd met a lady and was going to quit drinking. Her name is Erma Benfield. He said she's a wonderful person and is going to help him. He sounded excited."

"That's great!" Christie smiled broadly. "Good for him." Then she frowned. "But that should make you happy, not sad."

"It did," said Jana. "At first it all seemed wonderful. He wrote a few times, telling me how things were going at his Alcoholics Anonymous meetings. Then he and Erma got married. He sent me pictures of them with the justice of the peace at City Hall.

"Then he stopped writing. I've written him twice, asking if everything is okay, but he hasn't answered."

"Maybe he's busy," Christie suggested. "Maybe they're off on a honeymoon."

"I doubt it," Jana replied. "I think either he's started drinking again or my stepmother is intercepting my letters and not giving them to him."

"Why would she do a thing like that?" asked Christie in amazement.

Jana shrugged. "Jealousy? I've tried to be friendly. In my letters I've asked him to say hello to her for me, but I've *never* gotten any messages back from her. Maybe she doesn't want him reminded of his past." Tears brimmed in Jana's eyes.

"Oh, Jana," said Christie, stepping up to her friend and hugging her. "Have you thought about writing to him where he works?"

"I don't even know if he's got a job," replied Jana, wiping her nose with a tissue. "Besides, what would I say—Are you drinking again, or is your wife hiding my letters from you?"

"I guess you couldn't do that," Christie admitted.

"Now I don't know what to do," said Jana.

"Well, one thing you can do is try to forget him while you're on vacation," offered Christie. "There's not a thing you can do about it now. Who knows? Maybe there'll be a letter waiting for you when you get home."

Jana shook her head. "That's wishful thinking. But you're right," she said, smiling a little. "I'm on vacation with my best friends, and I'm going to enjoy it."

"Good!" responded Christie. As they headed back toward the bedroom to join the others, she added, "Let's start a pillow fight."

Jana laughed. "Great idea. I'll take Katie, you get Beth, and then we'll both jump Melanie!"

CHAPTER

6

"There they are," said Christie. Phoebe, Nicki, and Eleanore were waiting at the Green Park exit to the Underground. Christie looked at the three of them closely as she and The Fab Five approached. Had they gotten over their irritation at her, Melanie, and Beth?

"What kept you?" asked Nicki. "We've been standing here so long, I've grown moss on my north side."

Christie grinned. Nicki was back to her old self.

"We stayed up late last night talking and had trouble getting up this morning. Sorry we kept you waiting."

"I'm excited about seeing Buckingham Palace," said Melanie. "I hope we get a chance to see Princess Di."

"Whoop-de-do," replied Nicki, circling one finger in the air.

Melanie looked at her with a puzzled expression.

"Don't mind Nicki," volunteered Phoebe. "She's just not into castles. Her favorite things to see are the torture chambers in the Tower of London and Madame Tussaud's."

"Do you want to go by St. James's Palace before we go to Buckingham?" asked Eleanore. "It's on the way, and the changing of the guard is at eleven-thirty. We've got time."

"What's at St. James's Palace?" asked Beth.

"It's where the Queen Mum lives when she's in London," Eleanore told her.

"The Queen Mum?" asked Katie, looking confused.

"The Queen's mother," explained Christie.

"Well, why don't the British just say *that*, instead of Queen Mum?" asked Beth.

Christie held her breath as Nicki opened her mouth to say something, and then closed it. Whew, she thought, flashing her British friend a grateful smile. Nicki *is* on good behavior. Maybe everyone will get along a little better today.

"Unless Princess Di's visiting or something, I'm not interested in seeing St. James's Palace," decided Melanie.

"It might be fun," Jana said. "Maybe we could go there quickly."

"No," protested Beth. "Let's head for Buckingham Palace—"

"What's all the argie-bargie about, anyway?" interrupted Nicki. "If no one wants to see St. James's Palace, we won't go."

"It was just a suggestion," said Eleanore.

"It was a good one," Jana piped up quickly. "But I guess we'll skip it."

As they walked along in the direction of Buckingham Palace, Melanie glanced down a side street. "Oh, look. There's one of those cute soldiers in the red uniforms and big, black hats. Can we go see him? I want someone to take my picture standing beside him." She headed down the side street before anyone could respond. The others followed.

"Hi," called Melanie, approaching the guard. "Can I have my picture taken with you, please?"

The young soldier didn't respond. In fact he gave no indication that he even knew she was there.

Melanie looked up into his face, which was partially hidden under his tall bearskin hat. "What's wrong with him, anyway?" she asked.

Beth looked at the young man closely. "Maybe he's dead and just hasn't fallen down yet."

"No, he's not," said Eleanore, laughing. "The guards aren't *supposed* to talk to anyone."

"Do you think it would be all right if I stood next to him and had my picture taken?" Melanie asked.

"Sure," said Phoebe. "Tourists do it all the time."

"Be careful," cautioned Nicki, smirking. "If you make him smile or move, they'll put you in the dungeon at the Tower of London."

"Here," said Melanie, eyeing Nicki warily and handing her camera to Christie. "Would you take my picture?"

Melanie stood close to the soldier and smiled broadly. Just as Christie was about to snap the photo, the soldier raised his knee almost chest high and slammed his foot down.

Melanie jumped back out of the way, a look of fear and amazement on her face. "Wha . . . ?"

The soldier slapped his rifle, shifted it to the other side, and stamped his foot again.

The London girls roared with laughter at the look on Melanie's face. Nicki bent over, holding her stomach. Between peals of laughter, she managed to say, "I've got to have a copy of that picture."

Melanie looked wounded. "What'd he do that for?" she asked. "I thought he was going to shoot me."

Phoebe struggled to keep a straight face. "The guards do that at set times. You just happened to be next to him at the wrong moment."

Melanie looked up at the building they were standing in front of. "What is this place, anyway?"

"I'm not sure we should tell you," replied Eleanore, giggling.

Christie tried to break the news to Melanie gently. "Actually, it's St. James's Palace, Mel."

"Oh," said Melanie, looking embarrassed. Nicki, Eleanore, and Phoebe began laughing all over again.

Christie started to join in, but stopped when she noticed the look on Melanie's face. Her friend was usually able to laugh at herself, but this time Melanie seemed upset. The incident had really bothered her, and the British girls' teasing wasn't helping. Christie wished she could find a way to ease the tension between the two groups.

When the girls reached the wide avenue called the Mall that led directly to Buckingham Palace, they saw that people were starting to gather along the curb for the changing of the guard.

"We'd better find a place to stand before it gets too crowded," suggested Phoebe.

"Wow," said Katie, looking at the palace. "This place is only a little bit larger than my house."

"And that's just the back door," remarked Eleanore.

"Who's the statue of?" asked Jana, pointing at a huge statue surrounded by a pool of water outside the palace gate.

"That's the Queen Victoria Memorial," answered

Phoebe. "Victoria's regarded as one of our greatest queens."

"That's one thing I've always admired you British for," commented Katie. "You let a woman run your country."

"I hate to disappoint you, Katie," said Christie, "but the queen doesn't run the country anymore; the prime minister does."

"I know that," Katie said. "But at least there was a female prime minister when Margaret Thatcher was in office. In the States we've never had a female president or even vice president."

"The Queen's flag's up," observed Eleanore, pointing to a tall flagpole on top of the palace. "That means she's here."

"Isn't she always?" asked Beth.

"No," responded Phoebe. "Sometimes she stays in the country at Windsor Castle."

"Oh, my gosh," exclaimed Melanie. "Do you mean she has two palaces to live in?"

Phoebe nodded.

"Here come the guards!" cried Beth.

Down the avenue came soldiers on horseback. They were carrying swords and wearing brightly colored jackets and silver helmets trimmed in gold. It was a magnificent parade. When the soldiers had passed, the crowd moved out into the street behind them and followed.

"Everyone's going to watch the changing of the guard now," explained Christie. "Some of the arriving soldiers will stay to protect the palace, while the ones who were there will get a break. We can go and watch, if you want."

"Maybe we'll see Princess Di," said Melanie hopefully.

"Fat chance," replied Nicki. "Even if she is here, she won't be sticking her head out every five minutes to see if the post has come."

"We didn't expect her to," snapped Katie. "But we're not complete pessimists—like *some* people."

"Why don't we go to the Tower of London," interrupted Christie hastily. "We can use our travel cards and catch a bus. You guys have been wanting to ride a double-decker."

She turned to lead the way. Katie, Jana, Melanie, and Beth were right behind her; Phoebe, Nicki, and Eleanore followed them.

On the way they stopped by the Houses of Parliament so Jana could have her picture taken with Big Ben in the background.

Next they caught a bus and dashed to the upper deck. As they rode along the Thames River, Christie pointed out interesting sights.

"Those dragons at the ends of the bridges are supposed to protect London," she explained, pointing to statues of the mythical animals. "And that's the

Westminster Pier, where you can catch a sightseeing boat. Over there is where the Globe Theatre used to be. That's where Shakespeare's plays used to be staged. It's now being rebuilt."

When they reached the Tower of London, they stopped for sandwiches at a kiosk before going through the entrance gate.

As they paid their way into the Tower, Jana looked at the stone walls that stretched in two directions. "I was expecting to see a tower," she said. "This is more like a fort."

"It started out as a single tower," replied Christie. "The other towers and walls were added later."

Christie led the tour, showing her friends the Bloody Tower, where two young princes were imprisoned and murdered; the Traitor's Gate, where prisoners were brought in by boat; and the White Tower, with its torture chamber and chapel. Inside the Jewel House, The Fabulous Five oohed and aahed over all the huge diamonds, gold crowns, jeweled necklaces, and beautiful scepters in the royal collection.

When they had finished their tour, the girls piled onto another bus and went to England's Central Criminal Court, known as Old Bailey.

"I can't believe I'm standing in front of the most famous criminal court in the world," said Katie, looking up at the gray stone building with awe.

"Inside those walls some of the greatest trials in history were conducted, like Jack the Ripper's. Hundreds of spies and murderers and even some famous sea captains were put on trial here. This is awesome."

"Maybe you'd like to take her place," suggested Nicki, pointing up at a statue of Blind Justice that stood high atop the building.

"No thanks," retorted Katie. "But I would like to go inside and see if there are any lawyers or judges wearing white wigs and robes."

"Why don't you go on in," suggested Eleanore, sitting down on the steps. "I'll wait out here. My feet are sore."

"I'll wait here, too," said Phoebe, sitting down beside her. Nicki plopped down next to her without saying anything.

"We'll be right back," Christie reassured them. She knew the three of them weren't having much fun. They had been to all these places before. Still Christie had hoped they would join in explaining things to The Fab Five. Instead they were just following along, barely saying a word.

Inside Old Bailey Katie gazed up at the high ceilings. "Do you know that Old Bailey is built on the site of the notorious Newgate jail?"

"What's that?" asked Jana.

"A prison for debtors," Katie explained. "They

were thrown into dark, dank cells for not paying what they owed. Others were imprisoned for stealing something as small as a loaf of bread. Lots of people died in Newgate."

"What happened to it?" asked Beth.

"It was destroyed in 1902," answered Katie.

"Boy, are you lucky we didn't have a Newgate jail at home when you ran up all those credit-card bills, Beth," teased Melanie. "You'd have been in jail for life." The others laughed.

For the first time since they'd left home that morning, Christie felt relaxed. The Fab Five seemed to be more relaxed, too, now that Phoebe, Nicki, and Eleanore weren't around. She wished her two sets of friends would try to get to know one another. She was getting pretty stressed out over trying to keep both groups happy.

"Look, Katie, there's a female barrister, or whatever it is they call lawyers over here."

"Barrister's correct," Katie answered as the woman in flowing black robes and white wig that barely covered her real hair passed. "I think wearing those robes and wigs is so cool—it's such an old tradition."

Phoebe got up when she saw the five of them coming out of the building. "Seen enough for one day?" she asked.

"I have," said Jana. "I'm exhausted. You guys must be, too."

"I'm going to take a bus directly home," said Eleanore, dusting off the seat of her jeans.

"We'll see you tonight at Montague's, won't we?" asked Christie. The London girls assured her they would.

"Thanks for coming with us," called Katie as they headed off on their separate ways. "It was fun."

Christie winced as she heard Nicki say sarcastically, "Yeah, it was a ball."

CHAPTER

7

"I'm starting to feel at home in England," said Katie. "It's really easy to get around here, and there are so many things to do. I just might stay."

The Fabulous Five were sitting in Montague's on Tuesday evening. With them were Connie, Charlie, Davey, and the three girls from London.

"It sounds as if you birds had a right full day," remarked Charlie. He winked teasingly at Katie. "What with seeing Buckingham Palace, and all those other places."

"I'm surprised you could get McAfee to go along," said Davey, bumping Nicki playfully with his shoulder. "She's a bit of a couch potato, you know. Her idea of action is poppin' chocolate Olivers in her mouth while she's watching the telly."

"Chocolate Olivers?" asked Beth. "What's that?"

"A biscuit. I guess you'd call it a cookie," explained Nicki. She shot Davey a fiery look. "And I wouldn't talk, Mr. Wonderful. You're not exactly fit enough to compete in the Olympics."

"Hey," Melanie jumped in eagerly. "Did Christie ever tell you that there's a guy in our school who has won all kinds of Junior Olympic swim medals?"

Christie glanced at Connie, who was listening intently to Melanie. He knew Chase Collins was a swimmer and that Christie and Chase had dated. It was obvious that he had guessed it was Chase Melanie was talking about.

Jana quickly filled the silence that followed Melanie's remark.

"We had so much fun today. The parade at the changing of the guard was exciting. Is the Macy's Thanksgiving Day parade ever shown on TV here? Now *that's* a parade. It goes on for hours, and there are tons of marching bands and entertainers."

"And they've got these gigantic balloons made to look like Superman, Spiderman, Bullwinkle, Popeye, all kinds of cartoon characters," added Beth.

None of the British kids had seen it. Another awkward silence settled over the table.

"Care to dance?" Davey suddenly asked Melanie. "Someone just put on a Brain Damage song."

"Great!" Melanie jumped up.

Oh, no, Christie thought. Nicki watched the two of them walking to the dance floor and didn't look very happy. Christie wished that Melanie hadn't seemed so eager to dance when Davey asked her. Christie hadn't had a chance to talk to Melanie and Beth and tell them to be careful about how they responded to Davey and Charlie. She vowed she'd do it soon.

"We got our tickets for Brain Damage for Friday," said Phoebe, indicating herself, Nicki, and Eleanore. "My mum got them today."

"We haven't gotten ours yet," Connie replied, "but I'll have Neal call and reserve tickets for the three of us."

"I should have had *our* butler get our tickets," said Nicki.

"You've got a butler?" Jana asked her.

"Yeah," answered Nicki. "He doubles as me dad." The group laughed.

"How about you?" Charlie asked Beth. "Care to dance?"

"Absolutely, luv," said Beth, imitating an English accent.

"I guess our coves would rather dance with American birds," Nicki said to Eleanore.

"You've got nothing to worry about," Christie reassured her.

But as the evening progressed, and Beth and Melanie continued to dance with the boys, Christie knew Nicki and Eleanore weren't at all convinced.

"The guys asked us to dance, and we danced with them," said Melanie defensively. "That's all."

It was Beth's and Jana's turn to sleep in Christie's bed. They were propped up against the pillows with a large bowl of popcorn in between them. Christie, Katie, and Melanie were sitting in their sleeping bags, each with a smaller bowl of popcorn in her lap.

"Nicki and Eleanore ought to know we're not a threat," added Beth. "It's not as if we've been sneaking off with their guys. And besides, we'll only be here for a few more days."

"I know," replied Christie. "I've explained that. But think about how you'd feel if the situation were reversed. Melanie, if Shane asked Nicki to dance more than he asked you, you wouldn't like it."

"Probably not," agreed Melanie, "but if girls from another country were visiting for a few days and never coming back, I could put up with it. I'd want them to have fun."

"Oh!" said Katie, grinning. "So you're willing to lend your boyfriend to someone for the sake of international relations."

"I think Nicki, Phoebe, and Eleanore are also feeling a little left out," Christie replied before Melanie had time to retort. "I forgot to call them yesterday to invite them to come out with us. And it must be hard to hang out with a group of girls who have known each other for as long as we have."

Jana nodded. "You're right. We should definitely be more sensitive to how they feel."

"Okay," said Katie. "We'll be more sensitive. But I think that Nicki and the others should be more sensitive to us, too. We haven't been together for a long time. Besides that, when we leave we'll probably *never* be back. We want to have fun." Katie's voice dropped. "Once spring break is over, it will be a long time before we see you again, Christie."

"I've got to tell you," Beth chimed in, "I'm not used to Nicki's humor yet. When will I finally think she's funny?"

Christie gave her a wry smile. "She grows on you. It took me a while to like her, too, but she'd do anything for a friend."

"I guess I'll believe it when I see it," responded Beth. "Connie, on the other hand, is such a nice guy. You must really like him."

Christie sucked in her lower lip and thought for a

moment. "I do, but I still like Chase, too. Sometimes it's pretty confusing."

"Either way, you win," Jana told her. "They're both great guys."

"So what's the story with Chase, anyway?" asked Christie. "Is he dating anyone steadily?"

"No," said Katie. "He's dated Tammy Lucero a couple of times. And Heather Clark and Lisa Snow, but there's no one steady."

"Don't worry. We'll keep a close eye on him," Melanie reassured her.

That night Christie lay awake as the other members of The Fabulous Five gradually dropped off to sleep. Katie's comment about not seeing Christie for a long time had hit her in the pit of her stomach. After the girls left, she would be on her own again, without the rest of The Fab Five. And right now, with Phoebe and the others feeling a bit angry at her, that made Christie feel terribly alone.

If only I could find a way to make my two sets of friends like each other, she thought. That wouldn't solve all my problems, but it would help an awful lot. I know if they'd just get to know each other, we could all be good friends.

CHAPTER

8

*O*n Wednesday Christie called Phoebe, Nicki, and Eleanore to see if they wanted to go to Madame Tussaud's wax museum with The Fabulous Five. Phoebe said she had something else to do; Eleanore said her feet still hurt; and Nicki said she had better things to do, like her laundry. It sounded to Christie as if they all had had enough sightseeing. She was glad that her American friends hadn't heard Nicki's comment.

The Fab Five spent all morning at the museum, touring room after room of wax figures of famous people—world leaders, British kings and queens, American presidents, and rock stars like Elton John and Elvis Presley. Some of the wax exhibits were chillingly realistic—including prisoners chained to medieval torture racks in rat-infested dungeons.

On Thursday it rained and they spent the day writing postcards to friends and family at home, and listening to Christie's CDs. In the afternoon they had tea and hot apple pie at Mrs. Mansfield's and played with Jenny Fitzhugh. That evening they went to the Palladium theater and saw a musical. Beth was so thrilled with the play, she couldn't stop singing the songs from the show.

On Friday they all piled into the Winchells' car and drove to the Farrell estate in Hoddesdon.

"Good morning, Miss Winchell," said the Farrells' butler, Neal, when he opened the door. "Good morning, ladies." He bowed slightly to Katie, Jana, Melanie, and Beth. "Master Conrad and the others are gathered in the drawing room." He turned to lead the way.

Jana, Beth, Melanie, and Katie looked slightly stunned as they followed.

"Wow! Look at that," whispered Beth, pointing at the crystal chandelier glittering from the ceiling.

"Yeah, and look at all the portraits over the staircase," Beth whispered back. "The frames alone must be worth a fortune. Who are all those people, Christie?"

"Connie's ancestors," she replied.

Neal led them into a large room where Connie and the others were seated on sofas and armchairs. The paneled walls were painted a deep red, with pale cream trim. The ceiling was the same shade of cream with ornate woodwork accented in gold.

"Here they are," said Connie, getting up.

"*What a fantastic house*," said Beth, twirling around to take in the whole room. "I can't imagine what it would be like to live in a gorgeous place like this."

Connie shrugged. "I'm sure yours is as nice in its own way."

"*Riight*," said Jana with a wry smile.

Connie led the way out back. The riders walked through a formal flower garden bordered by green hedges that had been shaped into neat rectangles. Gravel paths cut through the gardens, and marble statues stood here and there.

"It's beautiful," said Beth, and the others readily agreed.

When they reached the stables, two saddle boys were adjusting the stirrups of a group of horses gathered in the yard.

Jana eyed the two-story brick stable admiringly. "Even the horses have it pretty good here. Would you mind if I moved in with them, Connie?"

He laughed. "I don't think you'd like what they eat. Have you girls ridden before?"

"Randy and I have gone a couple of times," replied Jana. Katie and Beth had also, but Melanie told him it was her first time.

"That must be Rigel," said Beth, pointing to a small, powerfully built black Arabian. Its tail and mane were long and creamy white.

"It sure is," replied Christie, taking the horse's head in her hands and laying her cheek against its face. "Isn't he the most beautiful thing you've ever seen?"

"He sure is," agreed Beth quickly. "And I like that horse, with the black spots, too. Can I ride it?"

"I'll help you mount," Charlie said, taking the horse's reins.

"But . . ." Eleanore started to say something, then closed her mouth.

"Here. Put your foot in the stirrup," Charlie instructed Beth. He put his hands on her waist and helped her up.

"Come here, Snowfall," he ordered a stocky white horse. Gathering its reins, he mounted, too.

"No one had better touch Sunshine," warned Nicki, stepping between Melanie and a bay-color horse. "She's mine."

Davey mounted a tall, gangly horse.

"Thanks a lot for the assist, Davey boy," said Nicki, pulling herself up on Sunshine.

"The dappled horse is gentle," said Connie. "Why don't you take her, Jana? And Melanie, you take Cleopatra."

Melanie eyed the horse nervously. "She's got such a big head. And look at her nostrils. They're huge, too."

The London girls laughed.

"That's the way they come equipped," replied Eleanore. "You can't get a horse any other way."

"Here. Let me help you," offered Connie, holding the stirrup for Melanie. "Wrong foot," he told her when she tried to put her right foot in the left stirrup.

"Ooops. Sorry," said Melanie. Eleanore giggled, and Phoebe put her hand over her mouth to hide a smile.

"Let her do it her way," said Nicki. "Maybe she prefers to see where she's been instead of where she's going."

Melanie frowned at her and changed feet.

"When you want Cleopatra to go, just dig your heels into her flanks," instructed Connie. "To turn, pull the rein in the direction you want to go, and when you want to stop, pull back on both reins. Got it?"

"I think so," answered Melanie, looking as if she wasn't at all sure.

"I'll stay with you, Melanie," volunteered Davey.

Connie looked around to see who still needed a horse.

"Katie can ride Sapphire," suggested Phoebe. "I'll ride Blackie this time."

"Eleanore, that leaves you," said Connie. "You take Buttercup." He handed her the reins of a beautiful gold-color horse.

"But he's *your* horse," protested Eleanore.

"No problem," responded Connie. "I want to ride Duke. He has been a bit testy lately. I need to remind him to mind his manners."

Connie mounted Duke and led the way out of the stable yard and across a lush green field spotted with grazing sheep.

"This is terrific!" Jana called to Christie as they rode along next to each other.

"Fun, isn't it?" Christie called back. It was good to see Jana's face flushed with excitement. It meant that she had, at least momentarily, forgotten about her problem with her father.

Connie led the group up a small hill, masterfully handling Duke, who balked at most of Connie's commands. As they turned onto a trail that cut through the woods, Christie noticed that Charlie was riding next to Beth and talking up a storm. Nicki and Phoebe were behind them, and Eleanore was next. She and Jana were following her.

Melanie was having trouble keeping up. Cleopatra was an easy ride, but the horse seemed to love wildflowers and was making frequent stops to sniff at them. Davey was holding back to keep Melanie company, except for a few times, when he couldn't resist letting out a war whoop and galloping his horse past everyone to take the lead. Then he raced at full speed back to Melanie, showing off by making his horse prance around her. Each time he did this, and passed Nicki, she gave him a look of disdain.

Christie caught up with Eleanore. "Ellie, I want you to know that I talked with Beth last night. She's not after Charlie."

Eleanore flushed. "It may be the other way around," she said. "Charlie seems to be taken with Beth."

"It won't do him any good," Christie assured her. "The Fab Five are going home the day after tomorrow."

"I've still got to deal with him after that," Eleanore replied.

Christie looked ahead just then and noticed a large oak tree. The riders had to duck their heads to avoid low-hanging branches. Christie pushed one away and let it loose carefully, so it wouldn't snap back and hit Eleanore.

She hadn't gone much farther when she heard

Davey give one of his yells, and expected to see him come racing by. Instead someone screamed.

Christie spun Rigel around to see what had happened. Melanie lay sprawled on the ground under the tree, and the horse was galloping away.

CHAPTER

9

*C*hristie pulled Rigel to a sliding stop as Davey was jumping off his horse. She was beside him in a flash as he knelt next to Melanie.

"Is she hurt?" she asked.

"I'm not sure," said Davey.

Melanie's eyes were closed, and there was a gash on her forehead.

Davey yanked off his sweater and spread it over Melanie as Connie and the others came stampeding up. Charlie took off after the horse.

"What happened?" yelled Jana.

In just moments they were all on the ground and crowding around to see.

"Give her room," said Connie.

He put his hand on Melanie's cheek, and her eyes fluttered, then opened. She blinked and looked from one face to the other staring down at her.

Shaking her head as if to clear it, she asked, "Did anyone see a runaway freight train?"

"Are you okay, Mel?" Christie asked.

Melanie struggled to sit up. Shaking her arms and legs to see if anything was broken, she said, "Other than having the wind knocked out of me and a sore head and rear end, I think I'm okay."

"Wow," said Katie, "you sure scared us. What happened?"

"It was my fault," Davey answered dejectedly. "I pulled a clanger. I was showing off, and my horse bumped Melanie's horse, who then took off. Melanie hit her head on that tree limb." He pointed up. "It was a dumb thing for me to do."

"It's okay," Melanie told him, smiling weakly. "I'm fine."

"It's not the first time you've pulled a clanger," said Nicki. "And I don't suppose it'll be the last."

Davey and Christie helped Melanie to her feet as Charlie brought Cleopatra back.

"Do you think you can ride?" asked Connie.

"Sure," answered Melanie, rubbing a sore spot.

Davey stayed by Melanie's side all the way back to the stable. As he helped her up the veranda steps,

Connie's mother and Neal came out to see what had happened.

"Oh, dear," said Mrs. Farrell, when she saw the wound on Melanie's forehead. "Neal, get the medicine kit."

In just a few moments Melanie's head was bandaged, and she was sitting in a chair on the veranda holding an ice pack against the side of her head. Pillows were stuffed around her to make her comfortable. In her lap was a plate of chocolate Olivers.

"Now if you need anything," instructed Davey, hovering over her, "just let me know."

Melanie smiled at him. "You're nice, Davey, but don't worry about me. I'm okay."

Nicki made a sour face, but held her tongue.

Shortly after that, Mr. Winchell arrived to take them home. As Mrs. Farrell was explaining to him what had happened, Phoebe drew Christie aside.

"What are your plans for Saturday night?" asked Phoebe.

"We're going to the Hard Rock Cafe for dinner with my parents," Christie told her. "We'll probably go to Montague's after."

"Are you sure you'll be at Montague's?" asked Phoebe.

"Pretty sure," replied Christie. "I haven't talked to my friends yet, but I think so."

"Do talk to them about it," said Phoebe. "What time will you eat dinner?"

Christie shrugged. "Five-thirty or six, I guess."

"Good," responded Phoebe. "If you change your mind about going to Montague's, let me know."

On the way home Christie thought about Phoebe's interest in whether she and the rest of The Fab Five would be at Montague's Saturday night. She felt very encouraged. It seemed that Phoebe, Nicki, and Eleanore finally wanted to be friends with Jana, Katie, Melanie, and Beth. Maybe things weren't as bad between the two groups as she'd thought.

"I'm so excited about seeing Trevor Morgan again." Beth was standing on her toes to see past Katie in the wardrobe mirror in Christie's room. She was putting on eye shadow as Katie was brushing her hair.

"He'll be surprised to find out we're in London," said Jana, spritzing perfume on one wrist and rubbing it against the other. "I wonder if he'll even recognize me."

"I think they should make more fashionable bandages," Melanie joked as she patted down the end of the tape that held hers in place. "This one doesn't go with anything."

"You're right," added Beth. "It's so . . . blah."

Christie laughed along with her friends. "Oh, I almost forgot to ask you. Phoebe wanted to know if we were going to Montague's Saturday night. She really sounded as if she wanted us to go. How about it?"

The Fab Five seemed to hesitate.

"We're still going to dinner at the Hard Rock Cafe, aren't we?" asked Beth.

"Yes," replied Christie. "I told her we might go to Montague's after that."

"Uh, I guess it's okay," said Jana. The others slowly agreed.

Christie was glad they'd agreed to go, but she felt a prickle of annoyance. Now that the London girls seemed more interested in The Fab Five, Christie's old friends didn't seem to care about being with the Londoners. Christie wanted to scream. She was getting so sick of balancing her two sets of friends!

CHAPTER

10

"Wow, what a crowd!" exclaimed Beth as The Fabulous Five filed through the gate near the band-stand in Hyde Park. "It reminds me of Central Park in New York."

"I love outdoor concerts," said Melanie.

"How are we ever going to find Phoebe and the others in this crowd?" asked Christie, scanning the nearby faces.

"We goofed," observed Jana. "We should have picked a place to meet. We'll just have to keep our eyes open. Maybe we'll get lucky."

"Let's hurry and try for a spot up front by the bandstand," said Beth. "Maybe Trevor will see us and wave."

"You've got to be kidding," scoffed Katie. "There'll be zillions of people, and he'll have spotlights shining in his eyes. How in the world will he be able to see us?"

"At least we'll be able to see *him* better," replied Jana.

"Everybody grab a hand and follow me," said Beth, taking Katie's hand. "I'll make a path."

As The Fabulous Five snaked between people, holding hands, Beth called out, "Excuse me. Pardon me. Lady with a baby!"

The crowd parted in front of her to let them through.

As they worked their way through the crowd, Christie looked in every direction for the London girls. Phoebe, Eleanore, and Nicki were nowhere to be seen.

"How's this spot?" asked Beth with a big grin when The Fabulous Five had reached a place not far from the bandstand. "Did I do good, or what?"

"You did fantastic," said Christie with a worried look. "But I just wish we could find the others." She didn't want her British friends to think they hadn't tried.

"We'll all keep looking," promised Katie.

They still hadn't found the others when the warmup band came on. As the music started playing, the audience began clapping and swaying, and it became harder and harder for Christie to see through the crowd. Finding Nicki, Phoebe, and Eleanore seemed hopeless.

When the band finished and the audience was waiting for Brain Damage to come on, Christie saw Davey's head bobbing toward them. He had spotted them and had a grin on his face. Christie could see Connie and Charlie behind him.

"Thought we'd find you birds right about here," said Davey. "How's the lump on the noggin, Melanie?"

"How'd you ever find us?" asked Christie.

"If it hadn't been for Davey's being six feet taller than everyone else, we might not have," teased Connie.

"Here they come! Here they come!" screamed Beth as Trevor Morgan led the members of Brain Damage onto the stage.

The Fabulous Five started jumping up and down, trying to get Trevor's attention. But with the shouting, waving crowd, it was impossible.

"Have you seen Phoebe and the others?" Christie asked Connie as Trevor introduced the band. "I'm worried that they'll feel left out if we don't find them."

"We've been looking but haven't spotted them," answered Connie.

Christie made a face. She hated it that they

weren't all together, but at this point there wasn't much she could do about it.

Brain Damage started their first song, and the crowd got right into it—swaying, clapping, and singing along. Trevor pranced across the stage singing the lyrics and teasing the kids nearest the stage.

"I wish Trevor would see us," Beth yelled above the noise.

"He always gets kids from the audience to go up onstage and sing with the band," said Melanie. "If he saw us, he might ask us to come up again."

"Hey, Mel," shouted Davey. "They're about to play the song we both like."

"Yea!" screamed Melanie, grabbing his arm and jumping up and down.

Davey put his arm around Melanie's shoulder, and the two started singing at the tops of their voices. The others joined in.

As the band played on, Christie forgot all about Phoebe, Nicki, and Eleanore. Connie took her hand, and the two of them looked at each other as they sang.

The band played song after song, and the excitement in the crowd lifted to a fever pitch. Finally Trevor Morgan started pacing back and forth across the stage, pointing to different people in the audience.

"*He's going to ask kids to come up!*" shouted Beth. "Oh, I wish he would see us!"

Everyone in the audience knew what Trevor was about to do, and the screaming and shouting grew louder and louder as he teased the crowd.

Beth and Melanie started jumping up and down and waving with both hands. "*We're here! We're here!*" they yelled.

Trevor was looking over their heads.

"We'll help!" shouted Charlie, grabbing one of Beth's arms and legs. "Get her other side," he ordered Davey.

Davey did, and the two of them hoisted Beth above their heads.

"*Trevor! Here! Here!*" she screamed.

Trevor saw her and looked as if he couldn't believe his eyes. He threw up his arms, then blew Beth a kiss. He motioned that he wanted Beth and her friends to come up onstage.

The fans standing near The Fabulous Five groaned with disappointment and shouted "*Lucky!*" as they cleared a path for Beth, Melanie, Katie, Christie, and Jana. The girls pulled Charlie, Davey, and Connie along with them.

"*Dudes and dudesses!*" Trevor shouted into his microphone. The cheering and shouting subsided to a dull roar.

"I want you to meet my fabulous friends from the United States. This is Beth, Melanie, Christie, Katie, and Jana, otherwise known as *THE FABULOUS FIVE!*"

There was a mixture of friendly cheers and boos.

"The last time I saw you, Beth, you were in an Indian costume," said Trevor. "What are you gals doing in London?" He stuck out his microphone so Beth could speak into it.

"We're on spring break and visiting our friend Christie, who moved here," answered Beth.

"Well, all *right*," said Trevor. "Glad you're here, and I hope you're having fun. And who are these dudes you've got with you?"

"These are our British friends," said Melanie. "Davey Hopper, Charlie Fenwick, and Connie Farrell."

A cheer went up from the audience.

"Okay," said Trevor. "I'm happy to meet you guys. Are you going to join in with The Fabulous Five on this next song?"

"I guess so," answered Davey, looking embarrassed for the first time that Christie could remember.

"What would you all like to sing?" asked Trevor as two stagehands brought out three wireless mikes and gave them to the girls.

Melanie suggested the Brain Damage song that she and Davey liked so much.

"Okay, guys!" Trevor shouted to his band. "Let's *do it!*"

The band started, and The Fabulous Five and the boys sang along.

When they finished, the crowd roared.

"ONE MORE TIME!" shouted Trevor, and the band started over, with The Fabulous Five, Davey, Charlie, and Connie singing at the tops of their voices.

By the time they sang the last verse, the crowd was going wild, and The Fabulous Five's faces were shining with excitement. Charlie was jamming his fists into the air. Davey grabbed Melanie around the waist and swung her in a circle. Charlie saw what he was doing, and grabbed Beth and swung her, too.

Connie looked at Christie with a big grin on his face and hugged her. She hugged back.

What a night to remember, thought Christie happily. Onstage with her best friends and the band Brain Damage in the middle of London, England, with thousands of people cheering. What more could you ask for?

She looked down into the audience swirling at their feet and saw Phoebe, Nicki, and Eleanore looking up at her. They didn't look happy at all.

CHAPTER

11

"*D*idn't I tell you they are *FABULOUS*?" yelled Trevor over the loudspeakers.

The crowd cheered.

"Stay onstage while we finish up," Trevor said to The Fabulous Five. "I want to talk to you."

After the performance was over, Trevor invited the girls and Connie, Davey, and Charlie into his private touring bus.

Charlie whistled as he looked around the opulent interior of the bus. The walls were finished in a dark paneling; the floors had thick carpeting; and soft, indirect lighting lit the rooms. Trevor was taking sodas out of a refrigerator and handing them out.

"I heard entertainers had fancy buses," said Charlie, "but I never imagined they were this nice."

"It's my home away from home," explained Trevor, sitting down on a long sofa and kicking off his shoes.

"So," began Trevor, looking from one member of The Fabulous Five to another, "tell me what you've been doing in London. I hope these blokes have been showing you the sights," he said, referring to Connie, Charlie, and Davey.

"Oh, they have," Beth assured him.

After they had been talking for half an hour, a man stuck his head into the room and announced, "We're ready, Trevor."

"Sorry, kids," Trevor said, standing up, "but it looks as if we'll have to cut our chitchat short. My manager's telling me it's time we left."

"Uh, Mr. Morgan . . ." said Davey.

"Yes?" replied Trevor.

"Could I, uh, like have your autograph?"

Trevor chuckled. "Sure. How about if I sign the soda can you've been drinking out of?"

"Fantastic!" exclaimed Davey.

"Mine, too!" added Charlie.

"I'll sign everybody's," Trevor told them, taking a marker out of a drawer.

"Wow," said Davey after they had left the bus. "I

can't believe we were in Trevor Morgan's very own tour bus. And look," he continued, pulling himself up to his full height. "He wrote here on my soda can, *To Davey Hopper, He's a big one*."

"You have to show that to Nicki," said Charlie. "It'll knock her bug crunchers off."

"Bug crunchers?" asked Katie.

"Her shoes," explained Christie.

"She'll claim I wrote it myself," said Davey. "But who cares? You guys can back me up."

We may all need to back each other up when we see Nicki, Eleanore, and Phoebe, Christie thought with a sigh. They weren't going to be happy about having been left out of things tonight. And Nicki and Eleanore especially weren't going to be happy about having had to watch their boyfriends onstage having fun with Melanie and Beth. Christie just hoped she didn't get a call from Phoebe telling her to forget about going to Montague's on Saturday.

"Phoebe?" Christie tried to keep her voice low. She was in the Winchells' study later that night and didn't want the other girls to hear.

"Yes?" answered Phoebe. Her voice sounded stiff.

"We looked all over for you before the concert

started," said Christie. "We couldn't find you. We should have picked a place to meet."

"You found Connie, Davey, and Charlie all right," responded Phoebe.

"We didn't find them," explained Christie. "They found us. And then we all looked for you, but the concert started. I'm sorry."

"Listen, Christie," Phoebe replied. "I know you want us to like your friends, but the way things are going, it's not easy, especially for Nicki and Eleanore. They're angry about Davey and Charlie, and I can't blame them."

"But Melanie and Beth aren't playing up to Davey and Charlie," protested Christie. "The guys are being friendly, and Melanie and Beth can't just tell them to go away."

"Well," Phoebe said, "Nicki and Ellie are furious."

"I know," Christie told her. "Look, Phoebe, I'll talk to Melanie and Beth again and tell them to back off totally. But maybe you can talk to Nicki and Eleanore and convince them to talk to Davey and Charlie about their feelings instead of blaming my friends." She softened her voice. "You three are my best friends in England. I really wanted you and The Fabulous Five to meet and get to know each other. If you would give them a chance, I know you'd like them."

Christie heard a sigh on the other end of the line.

"Okay," said Phoebe. "I'll try to talk to the girls. But you know Nicki. I'm not going to promise anything. Are you still going to Montague's tomorrow?"

"Yes," answered Christie. "We wouldn't miss it."

CHAPTER

12

*M*elanie and Beth were sitting at the kitchen counter eating when Christie came downstairs Saturday morning. "You guys sure got up early," commented Christie. "I didn't even hear you. Where are Katie and Jana?"

"They went out to buy souvenirs for Randy and Tony," said Beth.

"They did?" asked Christie, glancing at the clock on the wall. "The stores are hardly open. They should have waited, and we could have all gone."

"They didn't want us to have to follow them around," explained Melanie.

"I thought you wanted to get something for Shane, Mel," said Christie.

Melanie shrugged and looked into her cereal bowl. "I can get him something later, maybe tonight or at the airport tomorrow."

"The girls and I talked it over before you came down," said Christie's mother. "We thought we should go to the Hard Rock Cafe around five. That way they can buy T-shirts, we can eat, and you'll still have time to go to Montague's. Oh, by the way, happy birthday, dear." Her mother gave her a hug and a kiss.

"Yeah, happy birthday, dear," teased Beth.

"Happy birthday, Christie," added Melanie.

"Thanks," she replied. "Where's Dad?"

"He went to the office for a while," said Mrs. Winchell. "He'll be home in plenty of time. Want some juice, sweetheart?"

"Sure." Christie took the glass her mother offered her and opened the breadbox and took out a pastry. "Be back in a minute," she said, heading upstairs to the library. Her real reason for going downstairs had been to see where her friends were before she called Phoebe back.

"Did you talk to Nicki and Ellie?" asked Christie when Phoebe answered the phone.

"Yes, I did," replied Phoebe, "and they're not happy, as you might suspect. Especially Nicki. But since Melanie, Beth, Katie, and Jana are leaving tomorrow evening, they're willing to forget what happened.

"You know, Christie, part of the problem is, you're paying so much attention to The Fabulous Five, we're feeling left out. It's as if we're second-rate friends."

"*We're?*" echoed Christie. "Do you feel that way too, Phoebe?"

There was a moment of silence before Phoebe answered. "Yes, I do. Nicki, Ellie, and I are used to being your best friends, and now The Fabulous Five have come and taken you over."

"You're my best friends, too," protested Christie. "And The Fab Five are only here for a week." She lowered her voice. "I might never see them again."

"If your father gets transferred back to the States, we might never see you again, either," said Phoebe.

Christie sighed. "All I wanted was for you guys to like each other."

"Cheer up, Christie," said Phoebe, sounding warmer. "We're willing to try being friends if they are. We'll have fun tonight. You'll see."

After they had hung up, Christie sat staring at the wall, thinking. Phoebe had said she, Ellie, and Nicki were feeling left out, like second-rate friends. The Fab Five felt they had a right to monopolize Christie because they might never see her again after this vacation. That left Christie smack in the middle. It seemed as though there wasn't anything she could say or do to make things better for one group without hurting the other group's feelings even more. Tears filled her eyes. She had had such high hopes that this would be a great vacation. But instead it had felt like one long juggling act. She tossed half of her pastry in the wastebasket. Suddenly she wasn't hungry anymore.

"Mrs. Fitzhugh wants you to mind Jenny for about an hour," said Mrs. Winchell when Christie returned to the kitchen.

"When did she call?" asked Christie, puzzled.

"I talked to her earlier this morning," said her mother. "I forgot to mention it."

Christie groaned. "Couldn't she get someone else? The Fab Five are leaving tomorrow, and I want to spend as much time as I can with them."

"It won't hurt you to do it," answered her mother. "The girls can entertain themselves for an hour."

"But, Mom . . ."

"Aw, go ahead, Christie," Beth interjected. "It's just an hour. Melanie and I want to wash our hair, anyway. You won't be missing anything."

CHAPTER

13

"Hello, Mrs. Fitzhugh," said Christie.

Jenny was peeking out from behind her mother's legs.

Christie waved at the little girl.

"Meow," replied Jenny.

"I'm afraid she's still pretending she's a kitten," said Mrs. Fitzhugh with a look of resignation. "The only way I can get her to drink her milk is out of a saucer. Come in, Christie."

Usually Mrs. Fitzhugh was dressed impeccably when she was going out. Today she had on casual-looking clothes. "I'm not going out," she explained. "I've some office work I brought home that I need to do. If you'll keep Jenny out of my hair for an hour, I would appreciate it."

"Sure," agreed Christie, reaching down and picking up Jenny. "Let's go to your room, Jen, and see what you've got to play with."

Jenny started purring and licking Christie's face.

"I don't know why Mrs. Fitzhugh wanted me to mind Jenny," Christie told her mother when she returned home. "She said she had office work to do, but I heard her moving around downstairs the whole time I was there."

"Maybe she just needed a little relief," suggested Mrs. Winchell, smiling.

"Where is everybody?" asked Christie.

"Up in your room," said her mother. "Jana and Katie just got back."

Christie took the steps two at a time. When she opened the door to the bedroom, her friends' chatter stopped abruptly.

"What's going on?" asked Christie.

"We were just talking," said Melanie.

"Do you want to see what we got Randy and Tony?" asked Jana, jumping up.

Jana and Katie pulled shopping bags out from under the bed.

"I got Randy this," Jana said, holding up a white

shirt with a green silhouette of famous London buildings. Across the top it said "London" in beige letters.

"And I got Tony this," said Katie, pulling out a chain with a dragon on it. "It's like the dragons at the bridges that protect London," she explained.

"Did you get lost while you were shopping?" asked Christie. "You were gone a long time if that's all you guys bought."

"We did a little sightseeing on our own," replied Jana. "We were all over the city."

"Now we're sooo cosmopolitan," said Katie, feigning a bored expression.

"You are, are you?" Christie laughed. "You've only been in one of the largest cities in the world for a few days, and you think you know all there is to know about it."

"We're fast learners," said Jana, laughing.

Christie was glad to see that Jana seemed to have put aside worrying about her father and stepmother and was having fun.

"What's left on our list of things to see that we can get in this afternoon?" asked Beth.

"Well, there's the Old Curiosity Shop that Charles Dickens wrote about," said Christie. "It's fun and easy to get to. We can be back in plenty of time to go out to eat."

* * *

"We're near Hyde Park, aren't we?" asked Katie as Mr. Winchell parked the car near the Hard Rock Cafe later that afternoon.

Christie nodded. "It's right down that street."

"We're lucky," said Mr. Winchell, when they reached the restaurant. "Usually there's a line to get in here."

Inside the girls ogled the guitars and other memorabilia from famous rock stars that hung on the walls. Along one side of the restaurant was a counter and booths. The rest of the room was filled with tables.

"This place is neat," exclaimed Beth.

"What's a *pig* sandwich?" asked Jana, looking at the menu.

"One of the house specialties," replied Mr. Winchell. "It's roast pork on a roll. Try it—you'll like it."

"Since it's Christie's birthday, I think we should see if we can get them to bring us a cake with candles so we can sing 'Happy Birthday' to her," said Jana.

"I'll never forgive you if you do, Jana Morgan," replied Christie.

"I propose a toast," said Katie after the waiter had brought their food. "To Christie," she began, raising her water glass. "May she live to be a very, very old maid."

"Hey!" protested Christie. "I don't mind the old

part, but I do mind the maid part. I'm not going to drink to that."

"Just kidding," Katie assured her as the others laughed. "May you just live to be very, very old."

"That's better," said Christie. "Where are all my presents, anyway? I expected at least a truckload."

"Greedy, greedy," scolded Beth.

"We didn't get you any, because you don't deserve it," teased Jana.

"Actually we planned on your opening your presents when we got home," explained Christie's mother.

"I'd like to propose a toast, too," offered Mr. Winchell, raising his glass. "To The Fabulous Five, a great bunch of girls."

They clinked their glasses together.

"Happy birthday, Christie," they said in unison.

"We're so glad you girls could come," Mrs. Winchell told Christie's friends. "It's been fun having you."

"Thanks, Mrs. Winchell," said Jana.

The others nodded their appreciation.

As Christie looked at her parents and The Fabulous Five, happiness welled up inside her. It felt wonderful to have them all together.

After dinner they stopped by the restaurant shop so Katie, Jana, Melanie, and Beth could buy themselves T-shirts.

When they arrived at Queen's Pudding Square, Christie said, "I don't want to seem rude or anything, but would it be okay if I open my presents after we get home from Montague's? Phoebe and Nicki and Ellie are probably already there."

"It will only take a minute, dear," said her mother.

"Can we see the room in the basement where you built your science project first?" asked Jana.

"I'll show it to you in the morning," said Christie.

"Show it to us now," insisted Katie. "We have to pack tomorrow. There may not be time."

Christie felt a twinge of irritation. If they were late getting to Montague's, the situation with Phoebe, Nicki, and Eleanore would only get worse.

"Come on, Christie," said Melanie.

"It'll just take a couple of minutes," added Christie's father. "I'll drop you off at Montague's to save time."

Everyone seemed to be against her, so Christie shrugged and led the way downstairs.

Opening the door to the basement room, she felt for the light switch and flicked it on.

"*SURPRISE! SURPRISE! HAPPY BIRTHDAY!*" rang out a chorus of voices.

Christie was almost knocked backward by the shouting.

She was immediately surrounded by Mrs. Fitzhugh, Jenny, Mr. Fitzhugh, Mrs. Mansfield, and Mr. Dudley. Her parents and The Fabulous Five stood beaming behind her.

On the worktable where Christie had put together her project a few months ago was a large cake with candles and three cartons of ice cream. Plates, silverware, and napkins were arranged neatly in front, and a pile of gaily wrapped presents sat behind. Brightly colored strands of crepe paper crisscrossed the room.

"Happy Birthday, Christie," said Jenny, reaching out with both arms.

Christie took the child and hugged her close.

"You got tears in your eyes," said Jenny. "Why are you crying?"

"That's what you're supposed to do on your fourteenth birthday and your best friends throw a surprise party," answered Christie.

"Hey," exclaimed Mr. Winchell. "This is a time for merriment."

"Happy birthday, dear," said Mrs. Winchell. "I thought it would be nice if we had a small party for just family and neighbors before you went off to be with your friends."

"Happy birthday, dear," echoed Mrs. Mansfield, squeezing Christie's hand.

"Thank you, Mrs. Mansfield," said Christie.

Everybody sang "Happy Birthday," then Katie began cutting the cake and dishing out the ice cream.

"Now I understand a lot of things," remarked Christie as she took a bite of cake.

"Like what?" asked Katie.

"Where you and Jana went this morning, and why Mrs. Fitzhugh had me mind Jenny today. You wanted me out of our flat so you could wrap presents and decorate down here," Christie said.

"Wow, Christie really *is* a brain," kidded Melanie.

"Open the presents. Open the presents," urged Jenny.

"Jenny and I'll deliver them," said Melanie, taking the present on top of the stack and handing it to Christie.

When the presents were all unwrapped and placed on the table so everyone could see, Mr. Winchell raised his hands for quiet.

"I've got one more announcement," he said, "and this one is *very* important."

The room fell silent.

"While I was at work today, I received a call from Mrs. Davies, the lady I work for in the United States. She offered me a job at our corporate headquarters, coordinating mergers of offices similar to the one I've been overseeing here in London."

Christie felt as if time had just stopped. The only thing she could see was her father's face as he talked. What was he saying?

"Of course I immediately called Val," continued

Mr. Winchell, putting his arm around his wife. "We talked it over and decided we should accept the offer."

He looked around the room. "We feel sad about leaving such wonderful friends," but—he smiled at Jana, Beth, Katie, and Melanie—"we're happy about rejoining our other friends and family in the States."

Christie stared at her father in disbelief. They were going home. Going home to the town she had lived in nearly all her life. To Wakeman Junior High and all the friends she had grown up with. To The Fabulous Five.

CHAPTER

14

"*Y*EA!" A cheer went up from The Fabulous Five when they heard Mr. Winchell's announcement. They surrounded Christie and hugged her.

"Well, we certainly will miss you," said Mrs. Mansfield.

"Oh, yes," agreed Mrs. Fitzhugh. "You've been such good neighbors. We'll all be sad to see you go, especially Jenny."

Jenny looked confused over what the adults were talking about.

"When will you be moving?" asked Mr. Fitzhugh.

"In time for Christie to start school in the States this fall."

"That means you'll be with us in the eighth grade at Wakeman, Christie!" said Beth. "Boy, won't everyone be surprised to see you back."

"Especially Chase and Laura," Katie chimed in. "But for different reasons."

"Yeah, Laura will hate it that The Fab Five will be together again," said Melanie.

Christie's head was swimming. All of a sudden she had so much to think about. What would it be like to return to Wakeman after her year in England? She would be with all the people she had thought about and missed while she was here.

But she would also be leaving behind many new friends—Mrs. Mansfield, Jenny and her parents, Phoebe, Nicki, and Eleanore, and Davey and Charlie. The hardest part, she thought with a start, might be saying good-bye to Connie.

"I propose a toast," said Mr. Fitzhugh, raising his paper cup. "To our good friends the Winchells, whom we'll always remember fondly."

"Here, here," said Mrs. Fitzhugh. Mrs. Mansfield and Mr. Dudley applauded enthusiastically.

When The Fabulous Five walked into Montague's later, Christie's jaw fell. Sitting at a table and looking very unhappy were Phoebe, Nicki, and Eleanore. Connie, Davey, and Charlie were with them. So were Rebecca Stewart and Denise Hume from the girls' class at St. Margaret's.

In the center of the table was a very sad-looking ice-cream cake that had melted down at the corners. Next to it was a stack of paper plates and plastic forks. Party balloons floated in the air above the table.

Christie felt her cheeks flame with color. "I guess we're late," she mumbled.

Phoebe nodded glumly and didn't reply.

"Been out sightseeing, have you?" Nicki asked sarcastically.

"No, we . . ." Christie's voice trailed off. How could she explain to her London friends why they were late? Judging from their faces, there was nothing she could do to make up for ruining their surprise. She wanted to turn around and pretend none of this was happening, or better yet, melt right into the floor as rapidly as the cake was melting onto the table.

"Sit down, and let's cut the cake," suggested Davey.

"Spoon it, you mean," corrected Nicki.

"Whatever," said Connie, quickly passing out the paper plates. "Why don't we all have a piece, any-way?"

"This is awfully nice of you," said Christie lamely.

"Where were you?" asked Denise.

"We went to the Hard Rock Cafe for dinner and stopped by Christie's for ice cream and cake," babbled Melanie. "And guess what. Christie's father announced that the Winchells are moving back to the United States before school starts in the fall. Isn't that exciting?"

In stunned silence everyone at the table looked at Melanie and then at Christie. A furious expression clouded Nicki's face.

"*You had a birthday party at Christie's and now you think we ought to be excited about her moving back to the States?* I can't believe this!"

Melanie cringed.

A moment ago Christie thought things couldn't possibly get any worse. But they just had, and rapidly. "I'm sorry. We didn't mean to leave you out," she tried to explain.

Jana jumped to Christie's defense. "Mrs. Winchell is the one who thought the party should be just for family and neighbors. It's not Christie's fault."

"Are *you* family members or neighbors?" asked Eleanore, finally speaking up.

Jana looked taken aback.

"No, but we've known Christie a lot longer than you have," said Beth in an angry tone. "We grew up with her."

"Does that make you *better* friends than we are?" asked Phoebe. Then, turning to Christie, she said,

"We thought we were your good friends, too. But ever since they've been here, you've practically ignored us."

"That's not true!" protested Katie. "We asked you to go sightseeing with us."

"You totally forgot about us the first day," countered Phoebe.

"And when we did go with you, all we could do was follow you around and listen to you ooh and aah over things," said Eleanore.

Christie looked back and forth, from one girl to the other, as her two groups of friends stormed at each other.

"And now Christie's moving back to the States, so you can all forget about us," said Nicki.

"*Stop it!*" shouted Christie, abruptly standing. "All of you, stop it!" She was so upset, she was trembling.

The table went silent as everyone looked at her in surprise.

"I've had enough," she said. "I thought this was going to be the happiest week of my life, having my best friends from the United States and England all together. But it hasn't been. It's been a *mess*.

"You three keep saying you're being left out," she said, looking at Phoebe, Nicki, and Eleanore. "And you four seem to think that Phoebe, Nicki, and Eleanore shouldn't mind what we do, since we might never see each other again," she said to Katie, Melanie, Beth, and Jana. "Well, what about me?" Tears were starting to well up in Christie's eyes, and everyone moved nervously. "Did you even think about how hard this has been for me?"

She turned again to look at the British girls. "You know how much I missed The Fabulous Five. You were the ones who helped me to adjust. The Fab Five *have* been my best friends for years, and they mean a lot to me."

Then looking at The Fabulous Five, she continued, "And you knew that Phoebe, Nicki, and Eleanore helped me to get over my loneliness when I came here. They've also been my best friends." Christie's voice softened. "And now I'm going to have to leave them, the way I left you."

"I . . . I . . ." She fumbled for words. Not finding any, she turned and walked out of Montague's.

CHAPTER

15

"Christie!" called Connie. She heard his footsteps as he ran after her.

"Wait," he said, putting his hand on her shoulder.

They walked along in silence for a few moments before he spoke again. "You know, I wish I were as lucky as you."

"As lucky as me?" She looked at him incredulously. She had just told off every one of her best friends, and he was calling her lucky.

"Yes, you." Connie took Christie's hand. "You've got so many friends, they're fighting over you. But come to think of it, maybe that's not being lucky. Maybe that's just what happens when you're the wonderful kind of person you are."

Christie smiled and shrugged. "Thanks, but I'm not sure that I have any friends after what I said in there."

"Sure you do," he told her, taking her by the shoulders and turning her so they were facing each other. "They'll get over it. You'll see."

"I'm so confused, Connie," she said. "I don't know what I want anymore. I am excited about going back home . . . to the United States. But I don't want to leave here, either. I like England. I like all my friends here, and I like you a lot." She smiled up at him.

"I like you, too," he said. "But your going home doesn't mean we'll never see each other again. You and your mother can tag along when your father comes to London on business, and who knows— maybe I'll travel to the States with my father on a business trip. I could have done it before, but I didn't have any reason to go. Besides that, if you go to either Oxford or Cambridge, as you've been planning, you'll have to come back, won't you?"

Christie looked up at Connie. His blond hair was swept across his forehead, and his blue eyes seemed so warm. "Thanks," she said softly. "You're a really nice guy, do you know that?"

He bent down and kissed her. "Why don't we go back and see who's left at Montague's. Maybe we can act as referees, if anyone is still standing."

*   *   *

When they walked back into Montague's, Christie was amazed at what she saw. The Fabulous Five and the British girls, instead of standing toe to toe and shouting at each other, as Christie expected, were sitting around the table and talking as if they had been friends forever.

"Christie!" called Jana when she saw her and Connie walk in.

"She's back," Phoebe said. "Come sit down, Christie."

After Christie was seated, Katie said, "First, we want to apologize, Christie. We all knew how important this week was to you, and we ended up acting like total idiots, and we know it."

"I'll say," chimed in Jana. "We got carried away. I think we were jealous of Phoebe, Nicki, and Ellie because we thought we'd never see you again."

"And then I had to drop the fact that you're moving back to the States on them like a bombshell," added Melanie.

"After you left, we remembered how we felt when you moved away," said Jana. "It was as if we had lost a part of ourselves. We thought The Fabulous Five might be broken up forever. I'm sure that's how Phoebe, Nicki, and Eleanore are feeling right now."

"We told them all of this while you were gone," explained Melanie.

"And we had to confess, too," said Phoebe, smiling at The Fab Five. "We were just as jealous as they were. We resented their coming over here and taking up so much of your time."

"We should have remembered how important they were to you," continued Eleanore. "We didn't take time to get to know your chums, the way we should have. None of us was thinking about you."

"All this confessing is liable to make me cry, and then my eye liner will run," said Nicki. "The bottom line is, we've all acted like poops, Christie, and we're sorry."

As Christie looked around at the seven girls, she knew that Connie was right. She was lucky to have such fabulous friends on both sides of the ocean.

The following evening Christie and her parents drove The Fabulous Five to the airport. Phoebe's father had brought the British girls by to see them off, too. They all stood talking as they waited for the gate to the jetway to open.

As Christie stood watching the others, she started thinking about what had happened to her since she had come to London. For one thing, she had changed. For the first time, she had moved away from friends she had known all her life and found that you can't count on things staying the same forever. She had discovered what it was like to move to a foreign country and suddenly be the odd one, not understanding everything that was said or what people meant.

Now a huge part of her would be staying here in England. Some of her would stay with Phoebe, Nicki, and Eleanore, no matter how things turned out. Little bits of her would stay with Mrs. Mansfield, Mr. Dudley, and Miss Woolsey, one of her favorite teachers at St. Meg's. And bigger pieces of her, pieces that could never be replaced, would stay with Connie and Jenny. She quickly brushed away a tear.

Jana's voice suddenly broke through Christie's musing. "When Christie was going away," she was telling Phoebe, Nicki, and Eleanore, "we wanted to give her something special to remember us by. You know the bears that she keeps on her bed that look like us?"

"Well . . ." Katie jumped in. "We were hoping to leave you something nice to remember us by, so that you didn't only have bad memories of us."

"We asked Christie if it would be all right if we took the bears back and gave them to you," said Beth. "They mean a lot to us."

She opened her bag and pulled out the bear dressed in bright colors with hoop earrings hanging from its little brown ears. "This is supposed to be me," she explained, handing it to Nicki. "I want you to have it."

As Nicki reached out to take it, Christie noticed tears in her eyes.

"And this is me," said Melanie, pulling out her bear with the dress covered with hearts.

Eleanore took it.

"And there's no doubt who this is supposed to be." Katie chuckled, taking out her bear with the white wig and judge's robe.

Phoebe took it from Katie.

"Since there are four bears and only three of you, I guess you'll have to share mine," said Jana, pulling hers out.

Nicki wiped her eyes with her hand and fumbled in her bag for a tissue. "Darn you guys, anyway," she muttered, blowing her nose. "You're spoiling my image."

"One of these days you'll be getting another bear to remember me by," said Christie. "The one dressed in a tennis outfit that my father gave me."

Just then a voice came over the loudspeaker, announcing the boarding of The Fabulous Five's flight. Christie hugged each of them in turn. Then Phoebe stepped forward and hugged them, too. Nicki and Eleanore did the same.

Wow, Christie thought as her best friends disappeared down the jetway, pretty soon I'll be flying home, too.

Here's a preview of The Fabulous Five #32, *Class Trip Calamity*, coming to your bookstore soon.

"*D*o you think this outfit makes me look older?" Beth asked. She struck a sophisticated pose in front of a three-way mirror in the juniors department of Tanninger's department store. Katie, Jana, and Melanie looked critically at the off-the-shoulder black knit top and white denim miniskirt with tiny black polka dots.

"Yeah," said Katie, her eyes twinkling. "You look about forty-five."

"I'm serious," insisted Beth. "In another week we won't be seventh-graders anymore. We'll be *eighth-graders*, and there's a big difference."

"Especially if the vote passes to turn Wakeman into a middle school," said Jana. "Then they'll send the ninth-graders up to high school, and *we'll* be the upperclassmen."

"Right," agreed Beth, twisting in front of the mirror to check out the outfit again. "We'll be big deals, and all the little sixth- and seventh-graders will have to look up to us."

"It'll be great," Jana added. "But as much as I'm

looking forward to next year, part of me doesn't want this one to end. I can't wait for our big class trip to Ellis Island and the Statue of Liberty."

"Yeah," said Beth, giving her friends a sly grin. "And it's the perfect opportunity to practice being big deals."

Will Wakeman Junior High really become a middle school next year? And what will happen when four busloads of kids from Wacko go on their class trip? Are they as grown-up and mature as they think they are? Find out in The Fabulous Five #32, *Class Trip Calamity.*

Do you and your friends know the answers to these trivia questions about The Fabulous Five? Quiz each other to see who knows the most Fabulous Facts!

#31 Where do students at Wacko Junior High stick their gum in the morning?

#32 In book #7, *The Kissing Disaster*, what does Melanie's biology class dissect?

#33 What is Funny Hawthorne's real name?

#34 In book #29, *Melanie Edwards, Super Kisser*, which student from Wakeman gets kissed by one of the members of The New Generation?

#35 In book #27, *The Scapegoat*, which of Christie Winchell's new friends from London is descended from royalty?

You can find the answers to these questions, in the back of The Fabulous Five #32, *Class Trip Calamity*, coming soon to your bookstore.

Here are the answers to questions #26–30, which appeared in the back of The Fabulous Five #30, *Sibling Rivalry*.

#26 In The Fabulous Five Super #3, *Missing You*, what is the name of the horse that Christie rides in England?
Rigel.

#27 In book #23, *Mall Mania*, what is the name of Wakeman's new cable TV show?
The Wakeman Bulletin Board.

#28 In book #26, *Laura's Secret*, what is the name of Laura McCall's father's girlfriend?
Trudy.

#29 In The Fabulous Five Super #1, *The Fabulous Five in Trouble*, what video do the girls watch at Katie's house during the sleepover?
The Gorillas in the Mist.

#30 In book #5, *The Bragging War*, what is the name of the rock star Beth brags about?
Trevor Morgan.

ABOUT THE AUTHOR

Betsy Haynes, the daughter of a former news-woman, began scribbling poetry and short stories as soon as she learned to write. A serious writing career, however, had to wait until after her marriage and the arrival of her two children. But that early practice must have paid off, for within three months Mrs. Haynes had sold her first story. In addition to a number of magazine short stories and the Taffy Sinclair series, Mrs. Haynes is also the author of *The Great Mom Swap* and its sequel, *The Great Boyfriend Trap.* She lives in Marco Island, Florida, with her husband, who is also an author.